RITES *of* PASSAGE

Thomas J. Rice

RITES *of*
PASSAGE

FIVE IRISH STORIES

ISBN-13: 9780986221606
ISBN-10: 0986221600
Library of Congress Control Number: 2016909737
Barrow River Press, Andover, MA

Praise for Rites of Passage: Five Irish Stories

"Beautifully evokes a world at the same time nearby and distant: the Ireland of isolated villages, survival farming, deep poverty, desperation and violence - and of joy and generosity and love."

Charles Heckscher
Professor at Rutgers University and co-Director of the Center for the Study of Collaboration in Work and Society. Author of six books focused on labor-management dynamics, organization change, and the changing nature of employee representation. His latest book is titled, *Trust in a Complex World.*

"Told with sympathy and humor, the five Irish stories in Thomas Rice's *Rites of Passage* are of homeland lost and recovered, of fierce loyalties, of dashed and regained hopes, of betrayals and humiliations, of boys making their perilous journeys to manhood, of single mothers eking an existence out of stony soil, of the foibles and follies of small town communities, of grown men escaping the long shadow of childhood trauma. Although the themes of the book often have to do with irretrievable wrongdoing, the redemptive undercarriage is a celebration of characters' valiant struggles toward fairness and human dignity."

Eleanor Morse
Author of three novels, including: *White Dog Fell from the Sky.*

"Thomas Rice likes to say that he 'justs swings for the fences' when he writes fiction. In *Rites of Passage* he hits a towering home run that soars over the stands and out of the ballpark. These five essays are gems, nuggets that sparkle with mastery of detail, a clarity of language that brings rural Ireland in the 1950s into haunting focus with subtle psychological insights the way few Irish writers have. *Rites of Passage* puts Rice in the rarefied company of John McGahern. The first and last stories, "Rites of Passage and "Hard Truths," are little masterpieces."

Padraig O'Malley
John Joseph Moakley Distinguished Professor of Peace and Reconciliation,
John W. McCormack Graduate School of Policy and Global Studies,

University of Massachusetts, Boston. Award-winning author of 12 books; expert on democratic transitions and divided societies, with special expertise on Northern Ireland(where he played a central convening role leading to the Good Friday Agreement of 1998), South Africa, and Iraq. His latest book is titled, *The Two-State Delusion: Israel and Palestine – A Tale of Two Narratives.*

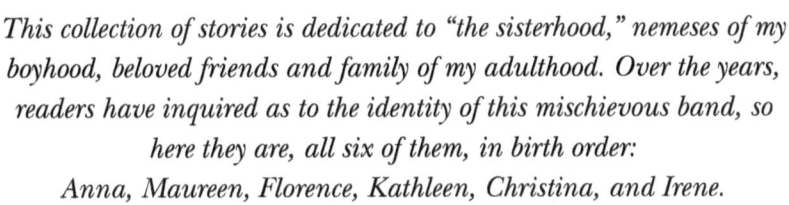

This collection of stories is dedicated to "the sisterhood," nemeses of my boyhood, beloved friends and family of my adulthood. Over the years, readers have inquired as to the identity of this mischievous band, so here they are, all six of them, in birth order: Anna, Maureen, Florence, Kathleen, Christina, and Irene.

CONTENTS

Rites of Passage · 1
Master Carney's Card School · 71
Dreams of Tramore · 85
All Souls' Day · 127
Hard Truths · 137

Acknowledgments · 187
About the Author · 189

RITES OF PASSAGE

Rites of Passage

Six hours on a cramped red-eye from Boston had Donovan in a foul mood—jumpy and irritable. He'd resisted this journey for eighteen years; never thought he'd find himself back in Ireland with this mission. Still, he reasoned, if things worked out, this would be the first and last time he'd have to make the dreadful trek. For a man who hated to travel, once was plenty. All the more reason to make this one count.

He'd been jerked from a semi-slumber by the screech of the landing gear on the Aer Lingus jumbo jet, slicing through the dense fog over Shannon airport. His wristwatch, which he'd set five hours ahead, showed "5:45 A.M., February 3, 2002." as he vaguely tuned in to the faux-British accent of the young stewardess prepping the passengers for landing.

Strapped pertly in her seat outside the cockpit, her short green skirt showing off a pair of long, sexy legs, the stewardess issued a litany of rote commands: "Please secure your tray tables and be sure your seats are in the upright position for landing. Check your seat-front pockets for personal…" Donovan tuned her out, reflecting on the pitiful irony of native social climbers still trying—and failing—to mimic the upper-class accent of their former British colonizers, fifty years after independence.

From his window seat near the front, Donovan smiled grimly at the familiar mosaic of green fields, brown fences, and silver streams decorating the luscious landscape of the Limerick dawn. As they came in for landing and taxied down the runway, he retraced—for the umpteenth time—the chain of events that led him to this "homecoming" moment.

It was the image of Archbishop Flaherty on national television, prostrating himself on the altar at St. Patrick's Cathedral in Dublin, that gave him the first cosmic nudge. He never thought he'd live to see a member of the Catholic hierarchy come forward like this—admitting the truth: *"Today I stand before you as a sinner to take responsibility for the abusers in our midst, to offer an apology to all who've suffered as a result, and to commit to making amends."*

Tears welled up in the anguished gray eyes as the Archbishop raised his open palms toward the crucifix, struggling to gain control, before going on: *"The abuses happened on my watch, in our chapels, in our diocese. I make no excuse, for I have none; I should have known. It was my responsibility to know, to protect the innocent. In that, I failed. I failed myself, and I failed all of you. I am guilty of willful ignorance, at best. No less a sin, no less abhorrent in the eyes of God. So today, I beg your forgiveness and ask Almighty God's forgiveness, as I pledge to do better, to be a more worthy servant, not just for today, or for a year, but for the rest of what time God grants me on this earth."*

With that, the old man fell on his knees, bowed his head, and prostrated himself fully on the altar, arms extended toward the granite crucifix above his head.

When Donovan saw the news coverage of what the media dubbed "The Spectacle at St. Patrick's," it was as though he was being offered a new lease on life, one without the shame, panic attacks, and loneliness—hallmarks of his existence since that awful May morning so long ago.

He still remembered—as if it were yesterday—the stained glass ovals and the crucifix lurching up and down through the fog of pain and terror.

Now here was the Archbishop of Dublin, one of the most powerful men in the Catholic hierarchy, offering a genuine, contrite apology. This, after everyone from the Boston Archdiocese to the College of Cardinals in Rome had closed ranks in ferocious defense of their pedophile brethren.

Donovan's next-door neighbor, Jimmy Brennan, put it best: "Jesus, Billy, those sonsabitches weren't only guilty of harboring known child molesters in their ranks—they were feeding 'em fresh meat, rotatin' 'em around to new, plum posts, keepin' 'em one step ahead of the posse." Jimmy was just giving salty voice to what was now common knowledge in every Catholic community from Ballydehob to Buenos Aires. Donovan had not responded. He didn't trust what he might have said, or how it might have landed.

That was before the rage took hold, propelling him across the Atlantic like a guided missile, only to find himself once again moving at a snail's pace through the customs queue.

A suspicious official pulled him out of line for a pat-down. Donovan groaned at the thought of another delay and the tedium of answering yet another set of questions designed to identify terrorists. He was tempted to blurt out, "What the hell is this! Do you think I'm the freakin' IRA?" Instead, he stood mutely, watching the old man—his hands arthritic and shaking—rifle through Donovan's faded shirts, slacks, underwear, and shaving kit.

After closely inspecting every nook and cranny of the luggage, the official finally turned to Donovan's passport. He stared at the photo taken almost ten years earlier and, with a slight stammer, asked, "How long have you been away?"

Donovan, in no mood for civility, snapped, "Well, as you can see, it's been eighteen years."

"Right, I see that, Mr. Donovan," the official replied evenly, "And what brings you home at this time of year, business or pleasure?"

"Oh, pleasure for sure," Donovan said flatly. "Pleasure it is. Isn't that what Ireland's famous for? Can't wait to get out of here to get started on the pleasure." The sarcasm was not wasted on the customs agent, who nodded and decided to let it go.

"Well, Mr. Donovan, I hope you have a grand time of it, and welcome home. Don't leave it so long next time." With that he smiled warmly, exposing a mouthful of blackened, rotting teeth, and Donovan suddenly felt ashamed of his own rudeness.

Following the green "AMAC" (EXIT) sign, Donovan was struck by how few things had changed in a quarter of a century. The white, three-leafed shamrock on the tails of the Aer Lingus fleet lined up on the runway; the leggy flight attendants, in their tight-fitting Kelly-green uniforms, rolling their travel bags as if on a catwalk, flirting with the copilots as they headed for a bit of R&R; and the pungent smell of sausages and blood pudding— he paused to consider indulging in a full Irish breakfast. All just as he'd left it back in 1987.

Even the brown bread and fried tomatoes—which Donovan had always found disgusting—were the same pulpy mess as ever. As was the sloppy service, which he'd forgotten until he waited in line for fifteen minutes before finally catching the eye of the tattooed short-order cook.

"Are ye all right there?" came the distracted greeting. With his blood sugar in his shoes, Donovan almost blurted, "Oh, I'm splendid; I love waiting in this stupid fucking food line at six o'clock on a wet, miserable, Irish morning. Why wouldn't I be all right?" Instead he smiled politely and said, "Right, I'd like a full Irish breakfast and a cup of coffee, white. Please!"

Another thing that hadn't changed—the coffee. Still Nestlé's instant; still undrinkable, even with milk and sugar. To think he once used to love this swill! He grabbed the tray of overcooked food and found a plastic table out in the hallway, near the exit, away from the chattering masses—all dug in on their cell phones and laptops.

On that score, the change was beyond recognition. He might have been on another planet. Revenge of the nerds, the chronic introverts who hate people, Donovan reflected.

He'd reserved a rental car with Curry's, and headed over the flyway to pick it up. The overbearing clerk—a dead ringer for Nurse Ratched in *One Flew Over The Cuckoo's Nest*—was all business, overdoing every detail to impress her wide-eyed trainee, a pale, acne-faced youth who looked not a day over fourteen.

Ratched was especially skilled in all the sleazy little sales traps designed to pad the bill. Aware that these were SOP for the industry, Donovan took great pride in frustrating her practiced efforts.

"Good morning, sir, how are we today?" Ratched began.

Tempted to challenge the use of "we" with his usual response— "What is this, the assisted living wing?"—Donovan restrained himself, again, determined to keep his mission in mind.

"I've reserved a mid-range car for a week. William P. Donovan is the name." He pushed the confirmation number and driver's license forward without being asked. Ratched asked anyway, still focused on impressing the trainee with her awesome sales prowess.

"May I have your confirmation number and driver's license, please? Right. Brilliant. All in order, I see. Now, Mr. Donovan, would you like an upgrade? Practically free of charge; how would you like a new Audi or BMW? Say but the word. These are all elite, executive cars that Americans of taste love to drive." She glanced at Donovan to see if he'd taken the bait.

"How much extra?" he asked, casually.

"It's practically nothing. I can look it up, but for you, we could do it for just thirty euro," she smiled in assurance.

"A week?" Donovan asked, knowing he had her.

"Sorry, that's per day. But as I say, these are elite cars for people like yourself who, ah, know…cars." Her reply trailed off, knowing the ruse had failed.

"No thanks. If you have a Vauxhall Astra, I'll take it." Donovan smiled at his success and winked at the blushing trainee, but Ratched was not done.

"Yes, of course, we can do that. Now, how about insurance? Irish drivers are a holy terror, you know, driving on the wrong side of the road and what have you. You wouldn't believe the cases we see here; fender benders almost every day. For an extra ten euro you can have full collision and …"

"No thanks," Donovan interrupted, "I already have my own insurance."

"Now, Mr. Donovan," Ratched insisted, "I doubt that your American insurance covers a rental here in Ireland. Are you sure of that? I'd hate to see you paying the full value of the car over a few extra euro. It could come to thousands, even for a side-swipe."

"I'm happy to live with the risk," Donovan said, his voice almost a shout. "Now may I have the keys, please?"

"Absolutely, Mr. Donovan. Just one last thing. Do you want to prepay the petrol? One less thing to worry about."

"How much will it cost me a gallon?" Donovan inquired, knowing the answer.

"Well, actually, it's nine euro a liter for whatever we have to add to fill the tank," Ratched conceded, again.

"No thanks. I'll bring it back full then. Are we done now?" Donovan asked this in a tone of exhaustion, which he was not faking.

"Yes, Mr. Donovan, just initial all the places you've declined our service offerings and sign at the bottom. There you go! Have a nice holiday. Welcome to Ireland." She smiled fleetingly, glanced at the trainee, and turned to the next customer.

Distracted by his battle with Nurse Ratched, Donovan made a wrong turn on the way out and had to backtrack past the rental counter to get to the remote parking lot. The trainee spotted him walking by, and blushed again, making his pale face a fiery red mass.

After a long search in the ghostly, fog-bound enclosure, he finally found space B-22 in Curry's lot; a red Vauxhall Astra was waiting for him, parked between two sleek Mercedes. The Astra looked puny and forlorn by comparison, and Donovan felt a brief pang of regret as he squeezed his 6'1"frame into the right side driver's seat.

After a brief scan of the gearing and miniature dashboard, Donovan nosed the Astra into the foggy darkness of the brand new four-lane Limerick motorway. Within minutes of driving precariously in the breakdown lane, Donovan sharply revised his impression that nothing had changed in Ireland. Sleek new cars, of all makes and models, swished past doing over one hundred kilometers—another change; speed used to be measured in miles per hour.

He spotted a few road signs, but they were impossible to read in the fog. All he knew was that he was headed for Kilkenny— so he was relieved to finally see a large green "N24," pointing due east, toward Waterford. Close enough, he thought. All he needed to do was get in and out of Killgarson village without drawing attention to himself.

The image of his home village, where it all began, filled Donovan with dread. It suddenly dawned on him that he'd given no thought to any practical plan of action. He'd simply acted on impulse, driven by the archbishop's confession and his own catharsis. But now what? Now that he was actually here and about to confront his molester, face-to-face? After all this time, the man might not even be alive.

The thought of a confrontation brought sweat to Donovan's palms. His hands began to tremble violently on the steering wheel, so he slowed the Vauxhall in the breakdown lane, emergency flashers blinking. Then came the familiar nausea, the tightening in his gut, the blinding dizziness. He pulled over to the first lay-by till the tremors passed and he could regain his composure.

It was time to make a plan, one that went beyond his eternal urge for revenge. "After all," he admonished himself, "You make a living as an anthropologist, teaching linguistics at St. Dominic's in Boston. Surely you can do better than this. Maybe you can even put some of that therapy to work, the stuff that never worked before." He recalled the well-rehearsed Steinberg's four stages—the four R's: remove, relax, reframe, recommit. Calmed by these reminders, Donovan stepped out of the car and took a generous lungful of pristine country air.

Pacing behind a hawthorn hedge, he imagined a conversation with Janet Woolf, one of his brightest graduate students—three thousand miles away in Boston—what if she were to come to him with this kind of dilemma?

"Tell me, Janet, what are your rational categories of action here? What place does linguistic theory have? What would Romsky *[his favorite American linguist]* suggest? How about the pragmatists, like Lucas Makoff and Katherine Duhring? Good. I see you've covered the range."

Enough theory. Who was he kidding? This was not a problem anthropology could solve for him; not today, not ever. It was time to reframe this whole mission, and not just to fit into some abstract, academic framework.

Donovan reminded himself of his dexterity and fame as a reframer of just about any practical situation. Language and its connotations—semiotics—was his specialty in anthropology. Challenge vs. weakness; opportunity vs. barrier; charity vs. justice; civil rights vs. welfare entitlement. His popular weekly column, "The Art of Reframing," in the liberal *Boston Commons*, was well known as fodder for right-wing talk-radio jockeys. They joked incessantly about the poor and handicapped being faced with "insurmountable opportunities," and the "character-challenged" nature of moochers and homeless people.

So how to reframe this one? He'd pondered this question *ad nauseum* over the years, but always dismissed it as absurd. He'd just be lying to himself. Why engage in a conscious act of self-deception? Was there any reframing of rape? Rape was rape: always brutal, vicious, and dehumanizing. There was no sugar-coating, no euphemism, that could ever change the hideous reality. That was the only thing Donovan was absolutely sure about over all these years.

Now, standing by the roadside as the sun burned through the morning fog, he wasn't so sure of that anymore. The facts would forever remain unchanged, of course, but this homecoming mission was not chipped in stone.

"How about this for a reframe?" Donovan asked the question out loud to the open field, just to hear how it sounded, "I'm not here to avenge a rape, but to reclaim my life, the one that was stolen from that fresh-faced eleven-year-old altar boy in Killgarson vestry twenty-five years ago!"

Hearing the words felt good, as if they had come from someone else—someone less involved. And wiser. This framing felt more doable, less violent, more in harmony with Donovan's cross-cultural training, discipline, and self-image.

Back in the Vauxhall, with the Galtee Mountains looming on the horizon, he still had no idea of how he might take practical action on this new idea of reclamation. As a professor, he was not accustomed to being concerned with practical applications.

The memory of that distant morning in the vestry now rolled in, crashing through his practiced defenses like a hurricane breaching a sturdy levy. Donovan fought off the urge to submit once more to panic. Instead, he smiled, took another deep breath, and got back in the Vauxhall, remembering his mantras: "Stay focused. Affirm. Visualize success. I can do this; I deserve better than this; I will do this. Yes, I can and I will do this!" With that little pep talk, Donovan calmly, almost cheerfully, eased the Astra back on the eastbound N24.

He tuned in to Radio Television Éireann—RTE—on the car radio to catch the local news. Instead, a DJ was playing a medley of Irish ballads. Jimmy McCracken and Nora White were singing a haunting duet of "Boolavogue." It was Donovan's favorite ballad of all time, sung by his favorite singers, and he marveled at his good fortune at finding it. He turned up the volume and sang the chorus at the top of his lungs:

At Boolavogue, as the sun was setting,
O'er the bright May meadows of Shelmalier
A rebel hand set the heather blazing
And brought the neighbors

from far and near.
Then Father Murphy from old Kilcormack
Spurred up the rocks with a warning cry: "Arm! Arm!" he cried,
"For I've come to lead you;
For Ireland's freedom we'll fight or die!"

Brilliant! Sheer genius, Donovan reflected, as he wiped away tears of joy and appreciation. The song was about a village just over the mountain from his home, a reminder of his tragic colonial history and the price his ancestors paid for their nation's freedom.

A few ballads later, the tears still flowing freely down his face, Donovan realized, with some surprise, how much he'd missed this music and the anguish it evoked, something he never felt for even his favorite American songs. He spotted the sign for Kilkenny, and his thoughts turned back to the ordeal awaiting him across the island in that sleepy little village.

Waiting to buy petrol in Clonmel, the last town before the Kilkenny border, Donovan retraced how it all began—with a dispute over a cheap penknife. Billy D., as he was known in school, had paid Mylie Doran, one of his pals in the third grade, a shilling for the knife—which Mylie had "nicked" from a contractor's toolbox. Though Billy hadn't taken the knife, he suspected that Mylie had, and bought it anyway, convincing himself at the time it was okay. After all, he didn't steal it, or participate in the theft. In fact, he'd paid Mylie a full week's allowance for it.

A few weeks later, his mother noticed the knife, which had disappeared from the toolbox of Mick Cash, a contractor who planted the wheat for local farmers. Cash had asked if she'd seen the pen knife—"a single blade with a red handle"—and she'd vividly recalled the conversation. "No, Mick, I can't say I've seen it. I'll keep an eye out for it, though. Maybe Billy was playing with it. You know how boys are..."

Mylie, she recalled vaguely, had been around the yard that day, too. He'd actually filched the knife, then sold it to Billy, hinting that it was "hot," but not how it came to be so. The secret was supposed to be theirs, and it remained so until a week later, when Billy's mother saw him making a hazel whistle with the red-handled blade.

"Where did you get that knife, Billy?" she asked abruptly, clearly angry.

"I found it in the yard," Billy replied, blushing and looking at his shoes.

"Don't you lie to me," his mother screamed. "What did I teach you about *lying*? And *stealing*? Is this the kind of boy I'm raising? I'm going to give you one more chance to confess before I turn you over to the garda."

At that Billy started sobbing and decided to come clean, "I didn't mean to do anything wrong, Mammie. Honest. I'd never steal, you know that. But I promised Mylie I wouldn't tell on 'im. He'll kill me if ya let on ya know. An' I don't even know for sure." Molly Donovan, relieved to find that she wasn't raising a thief— just a right eejit—relented.

"That's fine, Billy," she said softly, "I have no need to tell the Dorans about this. What Mylie does is their business; what you do is ours. But you have to promise me you'll confess this sin to the priest next time you go to confession. You're just as guilty as the thief in the eyes of God. He doesn't like 'fences'—that's what they call lads who deal in stolen goods—any more than thieves."

"Yes, Mammie," Billy had assured her, "I promise I won't be a fence anymore; I'll confess it next time I go to confession."

The following Friday evening he had his chance. Father McKenzie—the new curate in Killgarson—had pulled back the screen in the confessional, and Billy began as usual. "Bless me Father for I hav' sinned, in de name a de Father an' of de Son an' of de Holy Spirit."

Billy was immediately startled to see the priest peering at him through the tiny screen. The confessor was supposed to be anonymous, although this was pure fiction. His anxiety was exacerbated by the high-pitched register of the curate's voice:

"Now, tell me son, how long since your last confession?"

"A month, Father."

"And what do you have to confess?"

"Well Father, I lied ta me Mammie about stealin' a penknife. Actually, I didn't steal it, but I was a fence for it—dat's what Mammie says dey're called—an' she says I hav' ta confess it."

"A fence, is it? No, my son, your mother is wrong. You are not a fence; you're a thief, which God forgives only if you are prepared to take full responsibility for your sin—a mortal sin—and promise to never do it again."

"But I didn't steal it. I never would, Father. I paid for it wid me own allowance. But now I know it was wrong, an' I'm doing what I promised Mammie—confess ta being a fence, is what I promised her ta do."

"God will decide what it's called. He calls it theft. Do you understand? Barefaced theft!"

"Yes, but Father..."

McKenzie, fighting to control his temper, began to stammer.

"No more ifs, ands, or buts. If you continue this attitude of defiance, I will have no choice but to deny you absolution. Is that what you want?"

"No Father, I was just–" Billy never finished his sentence.

"THAT'S ENOUGH!" Father McKenzie shouted, in his high-pitched voice. It resounded the length of the chapel, turning all heads.

"Yes, Father. Sorry Father," Billy whispered, embarrassed and shaken by the curate's outburst.

"Is there anything else you wish to confess today?"

"No, Father. Dat's all dere is."

"Good. Now, for your penance, say ten Our Fathers and ten Hail Marys. Go in peace." McKenzie crossed himself, glared at Billy for a split second, and slammed the screen shut before turning to the next confessor.

Billy stumbled out to a gaping audience, crimson-faced, aware that the whole village would be buzzing with speculation on what he'd done to incur McKenzie's wrath, though the word was already out that the new priest had a short fuse. Billy crept into the closest pew and tried to focus on his penance, but all he could think of was that angry shout and the violence in McKenzie's voice.

Why couldn't he be allowed to explain? His mother had listened to him. Why couldn't Father McKenzie show the same courtesy? And why was he so sure God wouldn't know what a fence was? If his mother knew about these things, surely God knew, too.

McKenzie had been transferred to Killgarson after some trouble in his former parish; Billy had overheard the adults whispering about it one night when they thought he was asleep. Since his arrival—just a month before the knife incident—there was something about Father McKenzie that Billy hadn't liked. This was true for all the altar boys. Paddy Nolan, the oldest at fourteen, spoke for all of them: "I hate it when McKenzie comes out here. He's a right prick, if ya ask me. I t'ink he has it in for every wan o' us. He hates country lads; fucken Dub!"

That was the shorthand for urban priests—generic "Dubliners." In fact, all the altar boys were scared stiff of angering McKenzie—which was often over the slightest slip-up while serving mass.

This was in sharp contrast to the other two priests—Father Carey and Father Costigan, the parish priest—both older men and long-standing pillars of the community. They were always kind and courteous with the boys, praising them for the smallest accomplishments, fully aware that most came from fatherless homes, poverty, or both.

But for Billy, fear of ridicule didn't quite capture the feeling. There was something else—something sinister he'd sensed behind the thin lips, the stern, disapproving stare, the way McKenzie spoke in commands, the way he'd massage their shoulders with his soft, clammy hands as they lined up in the hallway before going out on the altar. Donovan didn't have a name for it; he just knew it felt creepy.

Like the other boys, he'd dreaded serving Mass when it was Father McKenzie's Sunday—which was only every third week, so it was bearable. Besides, he had no choice. On the bright side, he'd told himself, it was a major honor to be selected for the altar boys as a ten-year-old, plus the older boys had accepted him as an equal, and he'd made some pocket money on tips from the families at weddings and funerals. All told, except for McKenzie, being an altar boy was great *craic* (fun), and he was resolved not to let one bad-tempered priest ruin it.

It was three weeks after his confession when McKenzie's turn came around again. It was May Day, 1977, a day of celebration and high mass in the parish. Billy was not serving mass that Sunday and was looking forward to slipping out after the lengthy benediction to join his pals for a football game. He'd worn a new suit sent to him for his eleventh birthday—April 25th—by his older sister from London; he felt very posh when his mother put a white handkerchief in the left-side pocket. A regular fresh-faced toff!

That Sunday morning was a special May Day Mass, which meant benediction, always more uplifting than the regular ritual. Walking into the ancient stone chapel, with its scenes from the crucifixion, statues of the blessed virgin, massive granite urns, and stained glass windows in the vestry, Billy felt a sense of pride and belonging. This was *his* chapel, where he'd been baptized and where he was now serving Mass. Later, he would sing in the choir and perhaps be a priest here himself someday—if his mother had her wish.

In the hallway before Mass, Father McKenzie performed the usual creepy shoulder massages, whispering to Billy as he passed: "Wait in the vestry for me after Mass! We need a word." Billy froze with fear. What now? What else had he done wrong? All through the Mass, it was all he could think of, missing the litanies and many of the responses—lapses noted with glares from Father McKenzie.

At last, the benediction came around—which seemed in itself a week long—ending in a haze of incense and off-key hymns. The tasks of the altar boys were quickly done, everyone sprinting for the exit as if fleeing a prison. No one even noticed Billy sitting alone, pale faced, awaiting the verdict of Father Desmond McKenzie.

Over the next half-hour, Billy lived three lives and a hundred years of fear and guilt. What if McKenzie found out that he'd lied to his mother about other things—like the eggs that he ate without telling anyone, and the apples he'd stolen from Mrs. Dolan's orchard two years ago? Perhaps McKenzie had forgotten about him altogether.

As he was working up the courage to bolt for the freedom of the beautiful May morning, McKenzie strolled in with his vestments still on. Without speaking, he beckoned to Billy to follow him into the sacristy, the inner sanctum where the priest held his private prayers before services.

Entering the chamber, Billy noticed a large enamel basin of water in the prayer alcove. It rested on a chair above the kneeling cushion, and Billy didn't recall having seen it there before. McKenzie turned to face him as he walked in, appraised Billy's new suit coldly, and began: "I see you're looking immaculate in your new attire. But we both know you're far from immaculate, Mr. Donovan. In fact, I fear we have both become entangled in your sin, one which you have not repented and for which I should never have given you absolution. Now we are both sinners and must repent and atone together."

Billy couldn't believe what he was hearing. He was terror-stricken and groped for words, hoping to appease his accuser. "I know, Father, it was all my fault. I did steal the penknife. I'm a thief—I meant ta say dat—an' I'll say another penance if ya want me to. Sure, none of it was your fault. I'm to blame for it all."

McKenzie'd smiled a twisted little cat-like smile, waving off Billy's surrender. "I'm sorry. It's too late for that, I'm afraid. We have sinned together in the eyes of God, and so must repent together."

"But Father McKenzie…"

Billy never finished the plea. Suddenly, he'd felt his head explode from McKenzie's vicious slap, and he found his face buried in the cold basin of water, the curate's pudgy body pressed against his. The high-pitched voice had taken on a hoarse, urgent tone: "Shut up and repent. You must learn humility, to be cleansed from your vile habits and submit to the body and blood of Christ. You are going to learn about the true meaning of submission by the time this morning is done."

Billy had struggled for air, felt his lungs burning, but the clammy hands held his face under. Writhing in agony, Billy had managed to raise his head for a moment—a moment of blessed oxygen, only to be pushed under again, the clammy hands surprisingly strong.

Right before the room began spinning, Billy remembered thinking, "This is what death feels like," as his thoughts slowed, and he was sure he must be dreaming all of this. In the haze, he felt his pants slipping down, and wondered why, as though observing someone else from a distance.

A moment later, he knew this was no dream when the searing dagger of pain exploded through his body, inward and upward, as if he was being eviscerated. He'd tried to scream, but McKenzie, breathing heavily, rammed his head violently under water, before abruptly releasing the death grip to grasp his victim's torso with both clammy hands.

Billy remembered the first thing he saw as he came up for air—the stained glass window in the vestry door moving up and down. That was before he felt the blood running down the back of his legs. Oddly, a question had floated up about the blood stains on his new pants: What would he tell his mother? That was his last thought before the room went completely black.

When Billy came to, McKenzie was kneeling in the alcove, praying. He watched the bowed figure for what seemed like a long time, afraid to make a sound. Finally, McKenzie blessed himself, stood, and turned. "Feeling better, I see," he said, smiling brightly. "We always feel better after we repent and make our peace with God. Now you can go forth with full confidence that your sins have been forgiven and that you can rejoin the community of the righteous."

Billy said nothing, just stared straight ahead, dazed. He tried to stand but fell back down on the hard seat, only to feel a searing agony rack his whole body. He vomited all over the vestry floor, as Father McKenzie adopted the concerned attitude of a spiritual guide and comforter of the unwell.

McKenzie methodically cleaned up the mess, using the basin of water and the towels that normally covered the Eucharist. He turned to Billy and spoke in a whisper, as if with a co-conspirator: "Now then, young man, I know this cannot have been easy for you; it never is when we stray from the path and His way. But the Lord is all-knowing, all-seeing. He sets these trials in front of us for a reason—so that we can overcome them and grow stronger. What happened here today will remain between you and the Lord; I am a mere vessel for his commands. It is important, no, imperative, under pain of eternal damnation, that we never discuss our penance outside the walls of this chapel. It is God's law, not mine. You do understand this, yes?"

"Yes, Father, I understand. I won't tell anyone."

"Good; then we may leave in full confidence that all will be well. I'll drop you by your home on my way back to Killgarson House. My housekeeper will be very cross with me for being late."

On the drive, McKenzie was in high spirits, chatty in a way Billy had never imagined him to be. "You know, Billy, when I was a young priest in Mali—working among the Tuareg tribe near Timbuktu—young men scarcely older than you went through a series of organized ordeals called 'rites of passage.' A common one was circumcision—a cutting of the privates; another was one similar to what you've just experienced, with a respected elder of the tribe, like myself and the other priests in Killgarson."

Reaching for the lighter under the dashboard of the Austin Healy, he lit a Player cigarette, warming to his lecture. He took a deep drag and blew a perfect smoke ring before continuing. "You see, it's all part of growing up in these primitive cultures. We moderns have lost our traditional rites and rituals. But I can tell you from firsthand knowledge, they build character. A key to success is that the young men never complain about the pain or the healing; otherwise it fails."

He fell silent for a while, taking quick, nervous drags on the Player. Then came the conclusion: "They never, ever complain. They do suffer alone, in silence, to prove they're men. We need to reinstate rites of passage here in Ireland; we used to have them back in pre-Norman, Celtic days. The younger generation needs to learn something about that history, about character; about some of those old ways."

So that's what it was, Billy thought. He'd just been through a "rite of passage." Did McKenzie put other boys through this? Or was it just for sinners who didn't repent? Now that Billy had given his word not to say anything about it, things had to stay as they were. How would he describe it anyway? No one would believe what just happened—the brutality of the assault, the near-drowning, the...other thing, and the indescribable agony. Or the guilt and shame he was feeling for having been part of it; a bit like being a fence... *And what might this be called?* he'd wondered.

Driving at breakneck speed up the winding mountain boreen toward the Donovan farmhouse, McKenzie droned on with his lecture, and Billy tuned him out. As the farm came into view, he was reminded of more immediate concerns: What would he tell his mother about the blood stains on his new suit? How would he explain the lateness home from Mass? And the fact that he could barely walk or sit? This was all a jumble of confusion as he lifted his broken body out of the Austin and gingerly willed himself down the laneway to his farmhouse.

As he entered the kitchen, his mother's brusque greeting handed him a ready-made alibi: "What kind of child am I raising that goes and plays football in a new suit? Now look at it. Sure , I'll never get the stains out. What did ya do, roll in the mud? Go up and change, and don't you ever let me see you do that again!"

"I'm sorry, Mammie," Billy replied. "It won't happen again." Then he made himself scarce before she took too close a look.

That turned out to be the entire post mortem from his mother. Farm life had no time for extended interrogations or belaboring the obvious. There was work to be done and "more where that came from"—Molly Donovan's favorite saying. Cows, pigs, lambs, chickens, and turkeys all had their own insistent agendas, which they proclaimed loudly—all day long. A boy moping home late from Mass was just one more irritant among an unrelenting barrage.

Somehow, Donovan soldiered through the days and weeks after the rape without drawing attention. But for him, everything had changed—even the sound of the border collies. Their routine barking suddenly sounded mournful, ominous. People changed, too—looking at him differently, with suspicion and coldness. His teacher, Miss O'Brien, seemed more stern, calling on him at odd times as though trying to embarrass him in front of the whole class, which was not at all like her; he'd always been her favorite before that.

The following Sunday when McKenzie was due to say Mass, Billy suddenly took ill—he actually vomited in terror at the prospect of seeing his molester face-to-face—right before leaving the farmhouse. His mother took it in stride: "Billy, for heaven's sake,

I told you to eat more slowly. You're bound to make yourself sick the way you gobble your food. Let that be a lesson to you."

In school, Billy went from being a feisty, energetic leader to a pale, lethargic loner. First, his pals—including Mylie Doran, Jimmy Doyle, and Pete Fleming—abandoned him; just drifted away. The older boys began picking on him; then Mylie and the former pals, seeing an opportunity for sport, joined the parade. After school, "messin' with Billy D." became a favorite pastime, a sport all could play without fear of reprisal.

Most days found him fleeing the schoolyard, bloodied from punches or having his heels stepped on till they were raw—a favorite bullying tactic of his major nemesis, Brendan Crowley, a bull-necked, red-headed fourteen-year-old who'd failed the fifth grade two years in a row. It now seemed that Billy was fair game for every jackal eager to prove he was not at the bottom of the pecking order.

Finally, on a cloudless June afternoon, the last day of his fifth grade, feeling desperate and utterly alone, Billy decided to deny his tormentors further sport.

He ran away from school for the fifth day in row, sick of being taunted and slapped around by Crowley and his gang, all laughing and jeering. After the pack became bored with shoving him from one to the other, someone stuffed a rotten egg down his back and had crushed the shell to assure Billy D. would stink to high heaven, knowing he'd have a hard time explaining the stench to his mother.

Billy ran off as the hyenas convulsed in the laneway by the school, where they'd been waiting in ambush, just twenty yards from the chapel vestry where it all began just over a year before.

Billy took a shortcut home that day, avoiding the roadway. Crossing Tommy Dixon's farm, Billy collapsed under a giant oak in the middle of the field and wailed out loud, relieved at the solitude and the open space. He thought of ways to end his life—starve the hyenas and jackals of their prey. "Maybe I'll hang myself from a tree like this; stand on a bucket, then kick it away." He'd read about this in some comic book. "I suppose I could always drown myself in the Barrow; fill my pockets with stones, like Jimmy Doyle weighted the sack when he drowned that litter of mongrels." Even without the stones, he thought he'd drown quickly, having never learned to swim. "Or maybe I'll just run into Jack Fenlon's paddock and wave my red handkerchief at their huge Angus bull—everyone knows it makes 'em mad."

Still sobbing through these suicidal images, he never noticed Tommy Dixon walking across from the back gate until he heard a soothing male voice say: "Now, now…what is it that could make a young lad so gloomy on such a gift of a summer day? Sure, it wouldn't be dem hooligans back there in Killgarson school, would it?"

Overwhelmed at the sound of a kind voice, Billy poured out everything, except about Father McKenzie. "And I can't go back there anymore. I'd rather kill meself, I swear ta God, Mr. Dixon. I'm never going back there, and I know me mother will make me. But I can't take it any more…I just can't." With that, he'd dissolved into tears, sobbing against the oak, pushing the tears away with the back of his pale, thin fists.

"Now listen ta me, young Donovan," Dixon began. "I t'ink you're goin' at dis exactly da wrong way. If anywan needs killin', it's not you. Too strong a word anyways. But I t'ink ya just need ta be able ta stand up for yerself, teach dem boyos a lesson they won't forget. Are ya interested in some ideas along dese lines?"

Billy had smiled for the first time in months, it seemed.

"Yes, Mr. Dixon. But sure, Crowley and his pals are all bigger an' stronger than I'll ever be!"

"That's what I mean about yer going at this de wrong way," Dixon said calmly. "Did ya ever hear de sayin,' 'It's not the size of de dog in the fight, but de size of the fight in de dog'?"

"No, Mr. Dixon," Billy said, suddenly feeling better. "But I know it's true. Our little fox terrier, Nell, can whip dogs twice her size—she's that fierce."

Driving the Astra through the Tipperary morning, Donovan savored the memory of what one summer of practice, driven by a rich brew of fear and loathing, could do.

Leaning against that giant oak in Dixon's meadow on that rare June afternoon, Tommy Dixon made an amazing revelation. It turned out that he'd become a kickboxing amateur champion after he emigrated to New York in his youth. "Listen here, young Donovan, I can teach you a few things that will put that smirk on the other side of dem hooligans' faces." He said this with an intensity that lifted Billy's crushed spirit. "See, those ten years I was in the States, I made me livin' as a carpenter, but took up kickboxin' on the side. Sure it was a pure accident, how it happened." Billy hadn't said a word, incredulous that someone like Tommy Dixon—a big, strong man and a champion fighter—was finally in his corner.

Puffing on his crookshank pipe, Dixon retraced how it all came about in New York: "Kickboxing is one of the great traditional sports of the Orient; it was fairly new in the States at the time, in the 60s. I used to work out at this YMCA up near 42nd Street, and they had classes there run by a legendary Japanese kickboxing champ named Tohsio Tenaka. He later went on to train some of the greatest kickboxers of all time."

At this Dixon went silent for a moment, relit the pipe, and said quietly: "Don't get me wrong, young Donovan. I'm not braggin' or boastin' here, but Tenaka once told me that I was one of the most talented fighters he'd ever trained, including the Japanese great, Nai Shegei. I took it as a compliment; he wasn't wan for saying random blather. Very mild-mannered man. Never heard him raise his voice."

"Mr. Dixon, I never heard of anyt'ing like dat," Billy said. "Would you be willing to teach me some stuff about kickboxin'? We can't tell anywan; sure they'd just laugh at me."

"Don't worry about that, son—it'll be between us. Until it's too late for the bullies to do anything about it." Dixon said this with a smile and a mock punch to Billy's shoulder.

That summer, they'd worked out in Dixon's barn every evening after Billy was done with the chores at home. The deal was straightforward, and hard: Billy had to get in top shape by running at least a mile a day and skipping rope for thirty minutes, which he had to sneak in between his chores. He also had to lift weights, which Dixon did with him. And he had to practice on the punch and speed bags, at least half an hour a day on each.

After supper each night, they put on the boxing gloves and worked on specific drills for one to two hours. Billy learned all the kickboxing basics: classic stances, how to jab, cross, uppercut, and hook; how to bob and weave, side kick, and execute knockout moves, such as the roundhouse kick to the head, a nifty spin move practiced with Crowley's acne-scarred face in mind.

By the time school started in mid-September, Billy had grown two inches to almost six feet, gained ten pounds, and most important of all, had confidence that he could handle himself in a fight. His sparring matches with Dixon had grown competitive to the point that Dixon was often happy to call it a night.

Like going into a professional bout, Billy trained for the first day of the sixth grade, focused like a laser on one image: a punching bag comprised of Brendan Crowley's sack-like body.

But this was just one piece on Dixon's fighting chess board. Mostly he emphasized the importance of strategy in winning a brawl with no rules, which Billy was facing at Killgarson. "When ya take down the alpha in the wolf pack," Dixon declared, "the other curs turn tail and run. That's the t'ing about bullies: they're cowards at heart—can only dish it out; can't stand a fair fight. Make sure it's in public; make sure ya punish him and that ya beat him into submission. Right off! Never forget the element of surprise. They'll never know what hit 'em; they'll t'ink yer the same poor lad they stepped on back in June."

Coming back to school that first day, Billy was sick with trepidation. Tommy Dixon's advice only made things worse: "Take the fight to the big lad, Crowley, right away. Don't forget what I told you about the element of surprise. And be sure it's in public. The more witnesses, the better." Easy for Dixon to say. He'd been a kickboxing ace. Billy hadn't even had a single fight yet, and he'd be going against maybe half a dozen hefty farm boys.

The confrontation came immediately, but not as Billy had planned. He bumped into Brendan Crowley—literally—as the big redhead was rushing out of the loo, just before the first bell. Billy blushed, excused himself, and tried to step around his nemesis, but Crowley wasn't having any of it. "Hey, what de ya t'ink yer doin', gobshite?" Crowley snarled, reaching to rip Billy's shirt out of his pants—his habitual prelude to an all-out assault.

All Billy's fear evaporated in the face of Crowley's hated move. He forgot that he'd ever had a summer of kickboxing lessons; he forgot that Tommy Dixon had warned him this might happen, exactly this way; and he forgot about the element of surprise and the importance of making the fight public. Instead, he reflexively blocked Crowley's hand and smashed him with a left hook in the mouth.

For a split second, Billy saw confusion, then fear, in Crowley's amber eyes. But that brief glimpse of vulnerability quickly turned to rage as Crowley lowered his head and bull-rushed, pinning Billy against the stone wall of the loo, knocking the wind out of him. Crowley proceeded to gore him with head butts in the chest, cursing him all the while. "Feckin' little bollix. I'm going to KILL YOU! Ye'll be sorry ye ever raised a hand to me. Gobshite!"

Billy escaped from the vice-like clinch as Crowley made another blind lunge at his midriff, trying to tackle him. He missed, plunging his head into the stone wall, then turned toward Billy, dazed, hands dangling loosely. Seizing the opening, Billy remembered the punching bag exercises and moved in with a right cross, following up with a flurry of jabs to the nose and eyes of his hated assailant. Blood sprayed from Crowley's nose; his lower lip began oozing blood, and his left eye was beginning to close.

That's when Mr. Duggan came rushing into the loo, shouting, "What do you two think you're doing? Here we haven't even started school, and you're already into it. Get inside at once. I'll deal with you on the break."

"He started it, Mr. Duggan. I was just..." Crowley whined.

"Crowley," Mr. Duggan barked impatiently, "I doubt very much that Billy D. started a fight with you. But looking at your face, I'd say you might be careful the next time you decide to pick a fight with *him*. Serves you right, I must say. Now get inside."

On the short walk to the classroom, Billy beamed with satisfaction at the realization that all the summer work with Tommy Dixon had paid off. He'd won a fair fight with Brendan Crowley, something no one—with the exception of Tommy Dixon—would have believed an hour before. If this was what revenge felt like, it was one sweet feeling. He wanted more.

At the break later that morning, Mr. Duggan detained Crowley and Billy D. to hear their versions of the fight. He asked Billy to go first and listened with obvious skepticism as Crowley refuted Billy's version. "Mr. Duggan, Donovan's a liar. I was just mindin' me own business when he started pushin' me around outside the loo. Sure, I had to defend meself."

"All right, Crowley," Mr. Duggan interjected. "Your reputation as school bully is well established here, so I find your plea of victimization a bit rich. Here's what I'm going to do: Both of you will serve detention during breaks for the rest of this week. And if there is any more disturbance, I'll have to call in your parents for a conference. I won't have this school turned into a jungle where aggression and violence is the rule. Do I make myself clear?"

"Yes, Sir!"

"Good. I should hope not to hear any more about this."

Billy knew this was one hope that would not be fulfilled, not if he had anything to do with it. He hadn't spent a whole summer working his heart out just to let it all slip away with one brief skirmish.

Over the lunch break that day, Billy stayed inside the schoolhouse, determined to avoid Crowley and his gang, who huddled at the bottom of the schoolyard, plotting revenge. The Dolan twins—Jimmy and Frankie—were the most vocal of the underlings. "Why don't ye come on out for a little fun?" they yelled at the schoolhouse. "We forgot ta bring a football today, but sure you'll do instead." This inspired howls of laughter from the others: Horse Breen, nicknamed after his broad, horse-like face; Diarmud (Muddy) Walsh, who lived alone with his abusive, alcoholic father in a cottage up in the mountains; and Sean Dowling, another resentful fourteen-year-old, like Crowley, who'd been left back and hated school, like most of the pupils at Killgarson.

At the three o'clock bell, Crowley and the gang rushed for the door, as usual. Billy D. took his time, the nauseating fear returning as he contemplated what was waiting for him outside. He considered dodging out the back door, through Mrs. Finnegan's room, where he could avoid an attack for at least another day. But he knew this would only delay the inevitable and encourage the jackals even more. And besides, what was he going to tell Tommy Dixon? That he ran away from the fight? No, this was it. He'd have to face the music sooner or later.

As he slowly pulled on his schoolbag and started toward the door, Billy reminded himself of Dixon's advice, all he'd learned about kickboxing, and most of all, that he'd already won a fair fight against the brute force of Brendan Crowley.

This, of course, was not going to be a fair fight. It was going to be a brawl, maybe five against one, though he doubted Muddy or Dowling would have the guts to jump in; they were all talk, happy to let Crowley do their dirty work. Billy reminded himself what Dixon had coached: take it to Crowley, the alpha, first. Billy had done that already, to devastating effect—but without witnesses, so the lesson was mostly wasted.

That he was about to have his chance for witnesses became clear as Billy stepped into the laneway behind the school. Word of the fight had spread. Crowley had put the word out that Billy D. had jumped him from behind in the loo. Needless to say, such cowardly conduct cried out for punishment, which Crowley and his boys were now waiting to mete out. Most of the other pupils, drawn to the excitement—girls and boys—were lined up along the broad stone wall on the eastern perimeter of the schoolyard.

Crowley stood in the middle of the laneway, his gang behind him, blocking Billy's pathway. The burly redhead looked in no condition for a rematch. Both his eyes were swollen, mouth puffed up, and nose clogged with dried blood. He looked like someone who'd gone not just one heavy-weight round, but ten, and lost. Now he was back for more, trying to prove the morning's humiliation had been an exception.

Billy surveyed the pack, assessing his chances of taking Crowley out before the others had the courage to jump in. The Dolan twins each had hurling sticks, which they twirled like swords, mouthing ugly, jeering yelps. Horse Breen had his belt off, mimicking his violent da's weapon of choice for when his son displeased him. As Billy had rightly guessed, Walsh and Dowling were staying out of it. So far, so good. Now he knew what he was up against.

Billy dropped his schoolbag by the wall and removed his boots, slowly, placing them methodically beside each other. Another Dixon tip: get in their heads with preternatural calmness and strange, "foreign" rituals—like removing your boots, saluting the opponent, chanting, humming, even smiling.

The ruse seemed to work, because Crowley backed off as soon as he saw Billy's boots come off. "What the feck is this? What are ya, some kinda nancy boy?" Billy just took a deep breath, remembered the speed bag image, stepped forward into the imaginary ring and said, "Who wants it first? Come on, Crowley. Want some more from this mornin'?" Crowley, looking like a caged animal, glanced around at the gang before lowering his head and charging Billy, just as he had earlier. This time Billy was ready. He sidestepped the charge, stuck out his foot, and tripped Crowley, sending him flying onto his face in the dirt.

Horse Breen decided this was his chance. He came at Billy, swinging the heavy metal buckle in a vicious circle. Billy ducked the lethal buckle and came up with an uppercut to Breen's long jaw, but not before the swinging buckle caught him in the temple.

For a moment he was sure he was going to pass out; stars danced before his eyes, then he felt a warm stream trickling down his face, and he tasted his own blood for the first time, surprised at the salty sweetness of it. Breen was down on his knees, screaming, holding his jaw, his mouth bloody.

Crowley came back at him, undaunted. The crowd was cheering for Billy D., which he found surprising, but also comforting. Crowley repeated his one move—charge. Billy sidestepped again, this time landing a solid right cross to the redhead's bleeding nose, which opened a crimson geyser. Before Billy had time to follow through, Jimmy Dolan came at him, hurling stick raised, a murderous look on his face. "Ya fucken little shite, I'm going to end it right here. Ya had this comin'." The weapon coming at his head was a sharp reminder to Billy that he'd need more than his fists to survive this fight.

It was time to bring on the kickboxing.

Inspired by the thought of it, Billy spun away from Dolan in a smooth, bounding leap that brought gasps of admiration from the onlookers on the wall. He executed a roundhouse kick, catching Dolan under the chin and lifting him several inches off the ground as the hurling stick flew from his hands. Dolan landed on top of Horse Breen, who renewed his screams of agony, holding his injured jaw. Frankie Dolan, who was about to join his twin in the fray, backed off in alarm at the sight of his brother's slumping body.

Leaning against the wall, tasting his own blood from the nasty gash in his temple, and surveying the damage he'd inflicted, Billy savored the moment. He knew he'd won and that he'd never have to have this fight again. The sudden realization made him dizzy with relief and an almost unbearable feeling of exuberance. But it lasted just a moment before turning to an acute sense that something was missing—something essential to the success of the summer's work.

His long year of torment at the hands of Crowley and his pals now bubbled over into a towering, volcanic rage. He wiped the blood from his mouth and yelled at the top of his lungs: "Come on, yez bastards. Who's next? Which of ye gobshites wants to get his daylights shut? Who's the big lad now?"

When no one answered and no one met his enraged glare, Billy decided this was the moment to finish the job. Tommy Dixon's words came floating up, as if on a blinking billboard: "Make sure it's in public; make sure that ya beat him into submission." SUBMISSION. That's what was missing.

Homing in on Crowley again, who was holding his face with both bloodsoaked hands, Billy morphed from prey to predator. "How about it, Crowley? Want some more? Show me what ya got! Another charge, like a stupid bull? Is that it? That's the lot? Come on, ya don't want to let yer pals down now, do ya? Yer not afraid, are ya? It's just me, Billy D."

"Feck off, Donovan," Crowley blurted, through swollen lips. "I'll get ya whin ya least expect it, ya little bollix."

Big mistake. Feeling no mercy, Billy simply waded in, punishing his prey with vicious jabs and hooks, keeping an eye on the rest. No one came to Crowley's rescue, so Billy kept going. "I'm gonna teach you to shut yer gob! To cry uncle! I swear ta God, I'll keep beating you until you say the words, 'I give up.' Say it, gobshite. Say the words!" Crowley put his hands over his head, muttering something unintelligible. "I can't hear ya, gobshite. Louder! Let's all HEAR THE WORDS." Billy shouted this so that he could be heard all the way to the chapel, a full hundred yards away.

"Awright, awright!" Crowley pleaded. "For Jaysus' sake, Billy D., I give up! I GIVE UP!"

"That's the style," Billy said, and turned on the gang, who'd backed off down the lane. Emboldened and still bristling, Billy followed, taunting them with every step: "Anyone else want his feckin' daylights shut? Now's yer chance. How about you, Sean? Muddy? I haven't even warmed up on this tub o' lard. What are ya gapin' at, Frankie? Want to try yer luck with that hurl?" No takers. They just kept backing down the lane.

Billy D. put a hard eye on each of Crowley's forlorn pals, saw the visceral fear in their eyes, and kept stalking them, slowly at first, then charged into their midst, like one might a flock of geese, just to see them take flight. To his exultant delight, they turned as one and fled down the lane, several dropping their schoolbags in panic. He pulled up abruptly, laughed out loud, and turned back to the collect his belongings.

The crowd on the wall, completely in awe of what they'd witnessed, gave Billy D. a raucous and prolonged round of applause. He smiled, took a barefoot bow, put on his boots, picked up his schoolbag, and headed for Tommy Dixon's farm.

His last two years at Killgarson were among the best of Billy's life. His kickboxing prowess launched him to legendary standing in school, and, indeed, in the wider Kilkenny community. He continued his discipline with Tommy Dixon, growing bigger and stronger as puberty hit. With each passing month and with every fight won in the under-fourteen competitions, so grew the respect and deference of the Killgarson community.

Lady Luck smiled more than once on Billy's sixth-grade year. McKenzie was transferred in October, given a parish upland in north Kildare, a small village called Rathmore. Killgarson school had a going away party for McKenzie; Billy was chosen by Mr. Duggan to present a book of Yeats's poetry and to do a reading of Billy's choice.

He selected "The Song of Wandering Aengus" and read with full-voiced confidence:

I went out to the hazel wood,
Because a fire was in my head,
And cut and peeled a hazel wand,
And hooked a berry to a thread...

As Billy finished the reading, McKenzie listened with his usual icy detachment, cold gray eyes staring straight ahead, impassive. Seeing those amphibian eyes again up close brought the assault in the vestry rushing up, threatening to engulf him. Billy bolted for the toilet and stayed there until Mr. Duggan knocked and asked, "Is everything all right in there, Billy? Father McKenzie has to leave. Can you please come out to say tooraloo?"

"Sorry, Mr. Duggan," Billy blurted. "Tell him I'm really sick. Throwin' up. Say bye for me."

Mr. Duggan let it go. "All right, Billy. I'll make your apologies. Great job on Aengus there. We were all very moved. I especially love those last two lines...'silver apples of the moon; golden apples of the sun.' Pure genius, that Yeats!"

———◆———

Billy never saw McKenzie again, but never forgot him either. Not after he graduated from St. Aidan's in Kilkenny, with A levels across the board; not after he graduated from University College, Dublin with first class honors in social science; and not after his Guggenheim Fellowship and Ph.D. thesis at Columbia on "Cognition and Meaning in Cross-Cultural Context."

After earning his doctorate at Columbia, Donovan accepted a teaching post at McIntosh University, a small liberal arts college in Northampton, Massachusetts. Four years later, with the university's sponsorship, he'd applied for a green card and become a naturalized U.S. citizen.

Three well-received books, a coveted tenure track position, and a litany of honors and awards studded a distinguished academic career. Donovan was a competent, though never popular, teacher—criticisms like "aloof" and "never gives an A" were typical of student feedback. Yet he was a provocative keynote speaker at national symposia and college commencements. In his sixth year at McIntosh, he was granted tenure and promoted to associate professor of anthropology—the mark of a man on the move. Two years later, he was promoted to full professor and awarded the Noah R. Romsky endowed chair of linguistics.

His marriages were another story. After careening through three in eight years, he gave up. Luckily, he reflected, none of the marriages had produced offspring. The dreary, dysfunctional pattern was now well established; all the therapy in the world was not going to change it. After whirlwind courtships—the shortest taking a mere three weeks—there would be a plunge into marriage; a clean slate, all things possible, again.

Except intimacy. That was the hidden iceberg, always discovered too late, on which all three marriages foundered. Each woman knew the story. He'd made it his policy to lay the whole sordid McKenzie episode out on the table up front—by the second date, if not the first. He'd been in therapy since grad school, when he couldn't consummate his relationship with Gwen Norgren, a gorgeous classmate and the first girl he'd ever managed to seduce. Sort of.

He and his wives would work through that trauma, only to discover that the problem went much deeper than sex. On matters large and small, it turned out, try as he might, Donovan was closed to sharing anything beyond the most banal. Asked about his feelings, he didn't just shut down; he fled to an altered state, his emotional bunker, with familiar symptoms: knotted stomach, nausea, clammy palms—then full-blown panic. The only palliative was an immediate escape to fresh air in the great outdoors—field, forest, beach, mountain—unburdened by buildings or people.

With the passing of time and decades of practice, he'd managed an early detection system, but never made progress on the intimacy front. After over a dozen years and four different therapists, he'd finally stopped trying.

Now, at 36, already at the top of his profession, he believed that had been a good decision for him. He hadn't seen a therapist or slept with a woman since his last divorce, in February of 2000, five years ago this month. A good thing he hadn't been in Ireland all this time, he reflected, or he'd still be stuck in his first marriage. Mother Church still frowned on divorce, and that was the law—no separation of church and state in the Irish Republic. All contraception was banned here, even for married couples, though over 90 percent of Catholic women admitted to ignoring the sanction. Donovan smiled grimly at the double standard: an institution that nurtured pedophiles while sternly rejecting responsible family planning.

Donovan's three divorces had been amicable, no-fault affairs. No alimony. His former wives had all remarried affluent professionals; two were still in touch, had introduced him to their new husbands, and announced the births of their children to him. Donovan had reconciled himself to being single and celibate, limiting his social life to platonic relationships. No point in revisiting a watering hole that was a mere mirage, he mused, after a trip across the Mojave Desert. One of his colleagues in political science joked that Donovan had adopted a personal "Donovan Doctrine" of "no entangling alliances."

All of this presented Donovan with a maddening paradox. On the one hand, as a man who valued self-awareness, he accepted the fact that he was fatally flawed as a romantic prospect for any woman. On the other hand, he liked the company of women, still lusted after their beauty, missed the excitement of courtship, and hungered for intimacy.

Until he found it.

Yet he was tempted each time he saw an attractive woman and had to remind himself of his firm resolve: There would be no backtracking anymore, no last-ditch effort. Sex was a closed chapter in his life, like a sacred room that must be locked and abandoned for good, out of respect. It was not his to inhabit any more.

But the archbishop's repentance had challenged that vow, rekindling the prospect that the room might be revisited. Maybe, just maybe, a new subfloor might be unearthed. If the idea he was hatching could come to fruition, he might be able to go back, throw open those shuttered rooms, perhaps inhabit the whole house again—this time as a vulnerable, receptive mortal, not as a robotic academic with emotions encased behind a firewall of panic and self-loathing.

He passed through Roscrea, Tipperary—the fertile midlands—at noon, marveling that the drive had taken him two hours from Shannon. In the old days, it would have taken a full day to navigate the single-lane boreens, market towns full of livestock, cattle and sheep drives on every mile of road, and, of course, the county council workmen leaning on their shovels, chatting to kill the time, blocking traffic as often as possible. Happily, those days seemed in the past. Another major change, one he was deeply grateful for.

Closing in on his destination, Donovan stopped for petrol in Clonmel, bought a ham sandwich and lemonade at a local shop, and decided to treat himself to a picnic. He had a special place in mind and was delighted to find it still unspoiled. Hogan's Gap, they called it, a famous roadside vista overlooking Killgarson, his former village. He vividly remembered the spectacular quilt of verdant fields, silver trout streams, and perfumed, purple heather wafting off the majestic Blackstairs Range.

The rain stopped as Donovan parked the Vauxhall and stepped out, just in time to catch the rainbow that unfurled across the valley like a grand, welcoming banner. Sitting on a rock in Hogan's Gap, eating his sandwich, he could hear the farmers whistling to their border collies in the distance—the ewes noisily guarding their lambs against the intrusion—and a new, yet vaguely familiar feeling possessed him.

This was the home he'd erased from memory. Tears came again, soaking his shirt, as he saw, as if for the first time, the aching beauty of this precious valley he'd been forced to abandon.

In that moment, all of his noble intentions—to take the high ground, to forgive, to show compassion for his molester—were swept away in a tsunami of rage; of lust for revenge. Yes, revenge. He shouted it across the valley: "REVENGE!" He choked it down till it felt...right. Just. Revenge for his stolen childhood; revenge for the misery of three divorces; revenge for the lost beauty of this place; revenge for all the fresh-faced boys who, like him, stumbled mutely into the diaspora, broken and ashamed.

Now, the only question was: How?

With this newfound resolve spurring him on, Donovan headed for Glendunne, a small town just north of Waterford City, where he'd reserved a room at a distinguished bed & breakfast known as Glendunne House. It was part of a hotel chain called Fáilte Éireann—Welcoming Ireland—old mansions that had been converted to upscale but reasonably priced guest houses.

Checking in at the stately mansion, Donovan met his hostess, Mrs. Brennan—a lady in her mid to late sixties, with a warm smile and curly gray hair. He felt a restless anxiety as he asked if she could serve him a cup of tea now, and perhaps dinner later that evening.

"No problem, Professor Donovan, that's what we're here for. If there's anything meself or Sheila here"—she waved toward her daughter, an athletic-looking brunette in biking shorts, in her early thirties, with a gap-toothed smile—"can do to make your stay more comfortable, don't hesitate to ask. Just ring the bell, and we'll be right up." Sheila smiled shyly, nodding her affirmation as she turned toward the stairs, her elegant, athletic body on full display in her green biking shorts.

"Thank you, Mrs. Brennan," Donovan replied, "I've heard great things about Fáilte Éireann and Glendunne House in particular. I'm delighted to be here. How far is it up to Killgarson village from here?"

"I'd say now about forty kilometers. Isn't that right, Sheila? Not so bad, really. Now. Brilliant. We'll send up the tea and leave you in peace. It's grand to grab a bit of shut-eye after coming all the way from Boston. A frightful journey."

"Thank you, Mrs. Brennan," Donovan said, exchanging smiles with Sheila. "It's great to be here." He meant it, and was suddenly aware of that almost forgotten feeling of longing at the sight of an attractive woman.

Later, at dinner, Donovan was surprised to find three married couples, European tourists all, on biking tours arranged by Sheila Brennan—from Sweden, Germany, and France. All sang the praises of Irish friendliness, Sheila's tours, and Mrs. Brennan's cuisine.

They showed no curiosity about Irish history or culture, but they did imbibe Tullamore Dew till midnight, then wished each other slurred farewells and piper's invitations: "Come stay with us if you ever get to: Stockholm, Heidelberg, Carcassone. Hej da; guten tag; au revoir." Donovan shook everyone's hand and said, "Goodnight. A pleasure to meet you."

In the morning, they had all departed by the time Donovan wandered downstairs, still at half-mast, jetlagged. Three cups of strong Sumatran coffee and a delicious breakfast later, he was ready to launch. The time had come to disturb the sleeping beast—the one that had dozed for twenty-five years.

He drove toward Kilgarson, still with no plan, but with a very specific goal in mind, which involved a brief detour. He remembered The Trading Mart, just past Hogan's Gap, on a little side road two miles outside the village. It was a traditional animal market—called a "fair"—where local farmers brought their livestock to sell and barter on a set day every month. Donovan remembered it for an oddity: McCabe's Gun and Tackle Shop, where farmers bought shotguns and hunting rifles, as well as cheap handguns, like so-called Saturday Night Specials.

Donovan pulled up in front of the ramshackle building after about a half-hour drive. He looked up and down the road furtively, wondering if anyone would recognize him. Inside the shop, he felt a chill run down his spine at the sight of stuffed, preserved animals—foxes, badgers, weasels—decorating the walls. No one was in the shop, but a bell over the door brought an old man, in his late seventies, ambling from the back.

"Good afternoon," Donovan said nervously. "I was wondering if you had any small handguns for sale?" The old man looked at him quizzically through his thick glasses and said, "Well, it depends on what you need it for. We have a small selection, .32 and .25 caliber, Ravens and Desert Eagles. Run ya around fifty euro, with tax. Five rounds. What will you be using it for?" Donovan blushed and said, "Oh, just rats and small varmints. Damn nuisance. I get tired of trying to trap 'em."

"In that case, I'd go with the Raven. Nice, clean gun. Cheap ammo. I can give ya a box of fifty shells for ten euro and ya'll be all set." Without checking further with Donovan, he went into the back again and returned holding a snub-nosed handgun with a fine wooden handle that looked polished from use. He handed it to Donovan, who feigned a careful inspection, weighing it for comfort in his palm, spinning the chamber and fingering the trigger for comfort and fit to his hand.

"I'll take it," Donovan said flatly. "Also, that box of ammo you mentioned. It's fifty, right? That'll be fine."

Jack McCabe nodded his approval, put the gun and ammo into a thick paper bag and made out the bill with a shaky hand. He tore off the yellow copy, gave it to Donovan with his change, and said, "Happy hunting. I'm sure those rats will soon learn ta lave ya alone. They're real smart dat way." He smiled for the first time, revealing a toothless set of gums, then shuffled toward the dark rear of the shop.

Outside, standing in the deserted road, Donovan shivered at the memory of the creepy shop, amazed that McCabe hadn't even asked him for a driver's license or passport. He slid in behind the wheel, opened the paper bag, and inspected the gun again, liking the smooth feel, and was surprised at the rush of excitement—strangely erotic—from the snug fit in his hand. He filled the chamber with five bullets, spun it as he'd seen done in the movies, and pretended to fan the hammer with his right hand.

"Dirty Harry, move over!" Donovan muttered. "Go ahead, McKenzie, make my day!" He imagined the look on McKenzie's face as he looked down the barrel of this nasty little Saturday Night Special. With that vengeful thought firmly in mind, he decided it was time to give serious attention to the rest of his plan, now that a key piece was in hand. Intent on having some time to reflect, he retraced the road up to Hogan's Gap and sat down on his favorite rock to think the whole thing through.

It took Donovan a full two hours of intense reflection, weighing up the pros and cons of several courses of action, before he came to a decision. In the end, he got back in the Vauxhall fully resolved.

This was it. He was done with planning. After twenty-five years, it was time for action.

He drove into Killgarson without stopping in the village. Driving directly to the priests' house on the other side of the river, Donovan was struck by how small everything seemed compared to his memory of it. The road seemed narrower, the shops miniature, and the priests' house, which he'd always thought palatial, seemed small and drab.

He parked the Vauxhall on the road facing north, and knocked on the front door with its pretentious brass knocker, his breath labored and palms damp.

Moments later, a woman in her forties opened the door, smiled, and asked, "How can I help you?" Donovan smiled nervously and said, "I'm Billy Donovan. I was just wondering if Father McKenzie is still the parish priest up in Rathmore?" The woman smiled, nodded her head, and replied, "Hello, Mr. Donovan. I'm Mrs. Lawlor, and, yes, indeed he is. He's been in Rathmore now, for, oh—over twenty years. It's about an hour from here—near Curraknock. Take the N7 and get off at the second roundabout. You can't miss it." Donovan thanked her and left, then headed back into the village.

He parked in front of the schoolhouse and read the familiar block of granite over the front door: "Killgarson National School. Built in 1878." He smiled as he looked up at the front steps and the laneway where he'd first reclaimed his life and his dignity that September morning so long past.

Next he walked down to the graveyard, found his parents' tombstone, and said a few prayers—head bowed, but feeling no grief. He'd never known his da, and his mother had had no time for emotion. It started to rain, and he walked quickly toward the chapel, past the vestry where it had all happened. He entered the solemn stone building and walked slowly up to the altar, aware of the bloody crucifixion scenes—Stations of the Cross, as they were called—on each side of the aisle. He lit several candles for his dearly departed and knelt in the family pew, eyes closed in the dimly lit chapel, before he dared to look up.

Donovan finally opened his eyes, and there it was: the stained glass window in the vestry door—same as ever, except no longer bouncing up and down. He forced himself to relive the rape, in detail—the beating, the drowning, the nausea, the bleeding, the clammy-handed molester. He looked around the cold, austere chapel, with its statue of the Blessed Virgin and Jesus, whose eyes followed wherever you went. What would Jesus do in Donovan's shoes? Would he show mercy? Would he forgive such evil?

Donovan dismissed this line of reasoning with a shout: "To hell with mercy and forgiveness. This is me, Billy Donovan; I'm not Jesus Christ. And this never happened to him. No, justice will be done here. Des McKenzie is going to pay the full measure of his crime, right here on earth, right now. There can be no compromise with evil."

With that, he walked out of the chapel without a backward glance, and pointed the Vauxhall north toward Rathmore.

Driving faster than the speed limit, he followed Mrs. Lawlor's directions, which proved perfect, and arrived before noon at the ancient viaduct marking the beginning of Rathmore. It was his first time in the village, though it was less than an hour from Killgarson over the Blackstairs Mountains. Like dozens of villages he'd seen on the drive between Limerick and Waterford, this one seemed tiny, just a small cluster of shops on a narrow flagstone street. Thick moss clung to the gray stone walls surrounding the town; bored merchants paced outside their shops, glancing anxiously about, making small talk with each other. No customers seemed in evidence.

Donovan had noticed the same thing all across the island. The Celtic tiger—that universally heralded economic miracle—had suddenly morphed to a kitten, a tiny, sickly caricature of its roaring, fearsome self. The signs of devastation were unmistakable: boarded up shops; clusters of men standing around, smoking, looking pale and defeated; and "for sale" signs marking what seemed like every other colorful door of this postcard-perfect village.

He drove to the top of the street, where the shops and houses ended, and then noticed what appeared to be a secluded housing estate ahead. Curious, Donovan drove up to get a closer look. It turned out to be an opulent development, complete with a handcrafted iron gateway, showcasing a cluster of ersatz mansions, overgrown and abandoned, each fronted by gigantic Ionic columns.

Surprised to find such splendor in the middle of rural Kildare, Donovan drove through the massive gates, only to find a vast array of these abandoned behemoths—selling for millions at the peak of the boom—symbols of what he would later learn were only the most visible evidence of the anemic tiger: "ghost estates," as they'd come to be known all over Ireland.

At the last house in the cul-de-sac—a brown faux Victorian— one stone pillar had been erected at the end of the driveway, the second just tossed to the side, as if the builder had been forced to summarily flee the scene. No sense of symmetry, Donovan reflected.

He stopped in O'Connor's Grey Goose Pub on Davitt Street and ordered a lemonade from the chatty bartender.

"Can you tell me how I get to Father McKenzie's residence— you know, the parish priest?"

"About a mile out of the village on the Naas Road; he lives at Argyle House. A big white house with a blue door, right after the old schoolhouse at Clane Cross—on da right. Ya can't miss it."

"How will I recognize Clane Cross or the old schoolhouse?" Donovan asked, trying to keep a straight face.

"Oh, dat's right. Sure, yer not from around here, are ya? Let's see. Ah sure, like I said, ya can't miss it. If ya get to Clane, ya'll have gone too far, by around five miles." The bartender said this without any sense of irony.

It turned out that Donovan could and did miss Argyle House, not once, but twice. He got to Clane, doubled back, missed it again on the return trip, and eventually flagged down a tractor driver who escorted him all the way to his destination. Argyle House was set back from the road by a long driveway, barely visible behind a tall box hedge. It was a modest dwelling, with two cars parked in a gravel driveway.

By the time he got out of the Vauxhall in front of McKenzie's house, Donovan had rehearsed the plan so many times that it was grooved in his memory bank. He no longer had any sense of dread; no inkling of a panic attack. All he wanted now was to meet Desmond McKenzie face to face and begin to make the crooked places straight. He patted the gun in the right pocket of his gabardine overcoat and rang the doorbell.

Resolved and calm, he took a deep breath and waited.

A flurry of barking dogs came whipping around the side of the house, two terriers and a border collie—all showing off. They immediately turned friendly, wagging their tails, smiling. Donovan turned to face them, hands out, as he waited for someone to answer the door.

Eventually, as he expected, the housekeeper appeared. She was a white-haired woman in her late sixties, with lively gray eyes, wiping her hands on a faded blue apron while admonishing the dogs to quiet down.

"Sorry for the delay. I was just putting some scones in the oven for this afternoon's tea. I'm Mrs. Griffith, Father McKenzie's housekeeper. Please come in! Father is just finishing his dinner. Perhaps you would like to join him for dessert? It's apple pie and custard—very good."

"No thank you, Mrs. Griffith," Donovan replied too quickly, "I mean, I will join him, but not for dessert. I just wanted a word." The delicious smell of baked apples wafted across the foyer as Donovan followed the housekeeper inside.

"Yes, well, he's only now back from Dublin," she said. "And he's usually very tired after the trip and will need to rest soon. He has to be up for seven o'clock mass—every morning with the Sisters of Mercy, including hearing their confessions—of all things. It's a lot of work for him; he's here all by himself now, ya know. The parish is only half what it was five years ago. Emigration. It's killing us." The housekeeper seemed genuinely grief-stricken, and Donovan was at a loss for what to say. She pressed on:

"Back to where we were in the '50s and '60s. It's a crying shame, is what it is...losing the youth, the lifeblood of the country to foreign...Oh, who should I say is calling?" She seemed eager to keep talking.

"Thanks, Mrs. Griffith. Tell him Billy Donovan is here—wanting a word?"

Her eyes lit up with a glow of recognition.

"Billy D., it's you, isn't it? I thought I recognized you. There was somethin' familiar about yer face. Sure I remember the name well. Legendary kickboxer over in Killgarson, right? All the boys here picked it up; some of the girls, too. Ya were a hero to a lot of people, ya know, especially the parents. Kept their children off the street and involved in something they could burn all that energy on. As I always said to my Rory, I said..."

Donovan suddenly felt a panic attack coming on: stomach knotting up, sweat dampening his palms. Now that the housekeeper had recognized him, things were suddenly a lot more complicated than he'd bargained for.

He took a deep breath and refocused on the task at hand. "That's great, Mrs. Griffith. I really appreciate all this. But I need to see Father McKenzie right away. Can you please tell him I'm here?"

Mrs. Griffith, suddenly self-conscious, reflexively wiped her hands on the blue apron and started toward the dining room. "I'm very sorry, Mr. Donovan. Sure we're not used to such celebrities here in Rathmore. I'll just be a minute."

She returned and led him into the priest's study at the rear of the house. "May I take yer coat, Mr. Donovan?" she asked politely.

"Oh, no thanks, I'll leave it on, if you don't mind. I'm a bit chilled," Donovan replied quickly, sticking his hands into his coat pocket, feeling the gun for reassurance. He remained standing as Mrs. Griffith disappeared toward the kitchen.

Des McKenzie strode in, dressed in full clerical garb, collar, and black suit. Now in his mid-fifties, he still had a full head of hair, though it was turning gray, and he'd gained a lot of weight—complete with jowls and a double chin. He still had that air of detachment, too—or was it disdain?—that Donovan had feared and hated. Donovan recognized the familiar gait as he stepped forward to shake McKenzie's hand.

"Good afternoon, Father McKenzie. I wanted to have a word on a matter of some importance. I hope this a convenient time." The same limp, clammy hand he remembered reached out and went through the motion without expression. Donovan felt an overwhelming sense of revulsion as he met McKenzie's droopy, amphibian eyes. He withdrew his hand from McKenzie quickly, as if he'd touched something putrid. He felt the nausea well up, fought it back, and forced a weak smile.

"It's Professor Donovan now, I understand," McKenzie said, without smiling. "What a pleasure! What brings you to this neck of the woods? We're not inclined to have many distinguished alumni stop by our humble hamlet."

Donovan looked around the room, noted several photos of a young, smiling Des McKenzie, posing with African natives, and one with him holding a shotgun, his foot on a slain wilde-beest—Hemingway style—looking every inch the proud hunter. No other pictures of family or friends adorned the sparsely furnished room.

"Do you mind if we sit down?" Donovan began, "This may take a bit of time, and I've already been standing a while."

"Of course," McKenzie said pleasantly. "Please make yourself comfortable, my good man. You have my undivided attention."

Father McKenzie edged slowly around his large roll-top desk and sank down in his worn leather chair. He placed both index fingers in a V under his jowls, fixed his pale eyes on Donovan, and waited. Donovan took up the hard wooden chair facing the desk and window, looked directly into McKenzie's bloated face, and launched.

"I think you know why I'm here. I should have done this well before now, but better late than never, I suppose. I thought time would heal the damage you inflicted with your assault and rape of me in the vestry on that May morning in 1977." As he said this, he kept his eyes fixed firmly on McKenzie's face, who sat with a vacant expression, shifting his gaze to a spot on the roll-top desk.

"But it never has healed," Donovan continued. "In fact, it seems to get worse each year. The damage seems to be permanent, and my life has been irrevocably damaged. So I have a few questions for you, as my rapist, that might help me get some perspective, maybe even closure. At the very least, they'll satisfy my curiosity."

From Donovan's first word to that point, McKenzie had maintained a perfect poker face. The only tell was a slight reddening around his starched collar at "as my rapist" floated across the secluded study.

"What would you like to know, Herr Professor?" McKenzie asked, with a smirk, which inspired a murderous impulse in

Donovan that frightened him with its raw intensity. He paused, looking at McKenzie's disdainful face, and waited till his pulse stopped racing before speaking.

"Oh, a lot," Donovan said quietly. "For openers, why did you do it? And why me? Did you molest the other altar boys, too— Mylie, Noel, Sean, Bernie? Did you enjoy it, or was it to punish me for the knife incident? Did you ever confess it? Did you ever regret it? Did you think of yourself as a rapist, or do you now? Or as sadistic and violent? Or were you serious about that 'rite of passage' crap you ran out on me that morning? Oh, and yes— one more thing: Are you still molesting innocent boys and getting away with it?"

Donovan finished the barrage in a raised, accusatory voice and, oddly, as he did so, McKenzie seemed to relax—just as he had that May morning back in 1977, when he drove Billy home after the rape.

"Well, now, that's quite a list, Professor," he said, exhaling noisily. "I could never remember half of it—all so daft! Why *you*? Hmmm! That's the only one that matters, isn't it? That's the one you're REALLY interested in, isn't it?" This with red-faced vehemence, as he rose and walked around from behind the roll-top, pacing up and down, still without eye contact.

"Well, I'll tell you," McKenzie said, pacing faster back and forth in front of Donovan. "You were an arrogant little bollix who needed to learn a lesson. You were always a whiner, and I hate whiners; they are and always have been the bane of my existence. They never accept responsibility for their own shite, always the victim; it's always someone else's fault. Never theirs." As he said this, he finally met Donovan's gaze with a look of pure malice.

"My da was a whiner," he continued, turning abruptly to stand in front of the window, his back to Donovan. "He drank us out of house and home before leaving, but it was always mammie's fault. He told me so when I talked to him right after I was ordained. What a worthless coward! I hated the ground he walked on."

As if suddenly remembering that Donovan was still in the room, McKenzie faced him and said. "When you refused to accept responsibility for the sin of coveting your neighbor's goods, being a common thief, but still blaming it on...I can't recall that other boy's name?"

"Mylie Doran," Donovan prompted.

"Yes, of course, Mylie; it's been so long," McKenzie said. "Anyway, when you insisted on blaming Mylie, it struck me as high time you learned your lesson, one you wouldn't forget. The whiners may call it rape; we called it a 'rite of passage.' I'd seen these rites of passage work fine in Africa. As I told you at the time, the elders found it made men out of those boys. Thought I'd do you a favor as a fatherless boy, help you grow up in a hurry. I must admit, the water treatment was my own idea. Of course you fought like a demon, something I'd never imagined having to cope with. The rest seemed natural enough. Quite pleasurable, really. Is this the kind of detail you were hoping for?"

McKenzie said this as though he were selling vacuum cleaners to an interested customer, looking up for approval with an expectant air.

Donovan, incredulous and disgusted, took a deep breath, glanced quickly out the window, not trusting himself to look directly at the despicable figure in front of him.

"Oh, it's definitely along the right lines. Very helpful. Please carry on."

"What else were you curious about?"

"Who else? Were there others?"

"Oh, come now. Surely we're not here for prurient gratification. That's a personal matter, not likely to be a subject I discuss with strangers. Unlike you, Mr. Donovan, I've always accepted responsibility for my actions, and that's why I'm not playing the victim twenty-five years on."

Donovan—fighting an urge to whip out the gun and stuff it into McKenzie's smirking, ugly mouth, and blow those nasty brains to high heaven—took another deep breath, then suddenly had a jolting spark of clarity that felt like the lights coming on in a dark room—a true epiphany.

He smiled with relief at the new insight and the change of direction McKenzie's peroration had just inspired.

"Right, fair point," Donovan replied. "I could see where that would be irritating to a man in your position. I was just wondering if you ever reflected on being a rapist, or walked a mile in the shoes of the victims of your violence. But in a way, you've already answered that. There are no victims in your world. Right? Just... how would you classify all those people who have bad things happen to them through no fault of their own? Oh, I forgot... 'whiners,' right? You've already answered that. I'm a bit slow on the uptake, Des. Not like you; always one step ahead."

With that, Donovan stood, pausing before the massive desk. "Could I ask you one more favor?"

McKenzie, looking chipper, smiled and said, "Be my guest, Professor. How can I help?"

"I'd like to meet you in the chapel for confession in the morning," Donovan said. "I know you say seven o'clock mass, so perhaps before that. I have a plane to catch, but I really need to go to confession with you before I leave. I think it will help me to stop being a whiner, to get some closure and move on with my life."

McKenzie nodded solemnly, satisfied he'd handled this annoying situation with efficiency and firmness. He extended a clammy hand and said, "Music to my ears, Professor. Anything I can do for a star pupil. I'll see you at 6:30 in the confession box."

Donovan shook the limp hand, exchanged perfunctory smiles with McKenzie, and Mrs. Griffith saw him out, chatting away.

"I hope you come back and visit us soon. People won't believe me when I tell them I spoke with the famous Billy D. Did ya know they dedicated the recreation center in Kilkenny to Tommy Dixon? It's now the Dixon Center for Fitness and Martial Arts. You should stop by; there are several lovely photos of you with your trophies in the front lobby."

"That's good to know, Mrs. Griffith. How's Tommy doing these days? Is he still farming?"

"Oh, no, Mr. Donovan. He's been at Craigmore Nursing Home in Kilkenny for the past five years or so. A bit feeble, like all the rest of us." She laughed and said, "I'm sure he'd love to see you. He was always so proud of you. Craigmore's on the main road, just past Mt. Juliet Resort."

Donovan thanked her and left.

As he walked down the driveway toward the car, he felt an indescribable surge of energy and lightness he couldn't remember ever having felt before, like a man who'd just walked away from a terrible train wreck, one that could have maimed him for life.

On his way back to Glendunne, Donovan drove into Naas—a bustling commercial center—and found a camera store in the center of town. He purchased a backup battery for his digital Canon 510, checking with the salesman for how long it would hold the full charge.

He took a brief detour driving back to Brennan's B&B. He crossed the Barrow Bridge, pulled over at the lay-by, and tossed the gun and box of ammo into its brown, murky depths. He smiled as he watched the river gurgle on, undisturbed by its new secret, as if the deposit had never happened.

Reflecting on the near miss, he laughed out loud at the simplicity and clarity of his revised plan, feeling delighted that McKenzie had been so true to form—cruel and superior. This was going to make things so much easier than if his molester had become a repentant and humbled servant of God.

Donovan got back in the Vauxhall. He gazed at the river's calming flow and opened the car windows, savoring the delicate scent of the heather blowing in from the Blackstairs, blending with the lilac hedge he'd parked beside. He tuned in the radio, searching for Radio Éireann's traditional ballad program. He was delighted to find Nora White again, this time singing "The Rose of Allendale"—another of his all-time favorites, sung by a world class voice, he thought. He turned on the recorder on his smartphone and tested it to make sure it was working—reminding himself he was going to need this later if his plan was to succeed.

He played back "The Rose of Allendale" on the voice recorder, pleased that he'd captured such a fine rendition. It was good to be home, he reflected, in his own culture, singing the beloved chorus at the top of his lungs—a free man seeking justice, not a murderous stalker with a Saturday Night Special in his gabardine pocket. He smiled at the reframing, started the car, and stepped on the accelerator, hugging the narrow curves with the Astra's bumper, rallying at breakneck speed, all the way to Glendunne House.

As Donovan pulled into the driveway, Sheila Brennan, his host's daughter, drove in behind him in a BMW, several bikes strapped to the roof-rack. She waved to him, brunette curls swirling around her high cheekbones. As she reached to unload the bikes, still in her green shorts, it struck Donovan that his first impression was right—this woman was absolutely gorgeous. She had the kind of rare Celtic beauty seen only on travel brochures and in videos sponsored by the tourist board. And her gap-toothed smile was erotic beyond words.

"Can I give you a hand with the bikes?" he ventured, riveted on the green eyes and the enticing smile.

"Sure," she said, "Maybe I can inspire you to come on one of our tours. They're great craic, you know. We make all the arrangements—all you have to do is pedal."

"Well, that's quite an offer," Donovan said. "What are you doing for dinner tonight? I need a tour guide to sort out the complex cuisine of Kilkenny."

"You mean the choice between varieties of fish n' chips," she said, laughing. "I'd love to have dinner with you, and I know just the place—right here. Mother is away for the night. You can help me cook; fresh salmon okay?"

"It's my absolute favorite," Donovan exulted. "I'll nip into Cavanagh's and get us some wine. What do you like?"

"Oh, any Chardonnay is fine. I'm not fussy. They have a good selection. You can't go wrong."

Before stopping at the wine store, Donovan went back to his room, dialed a Dublin number, and waited. No one picked up. After he'd showered and changed for dinner, he called again, this time with more luck. "Hello, Declan," he said, "you'll never guess who this is! No clue? It's Billy Donovan—down home on a bit of business." They chatted briefly, ending with an assurance from Donovan. "No, Declan. You have my word on it. Tell your editor to hold a full page. You're guaranteed to fill it. This'll make international headlines. Can't hurt your career one bit. Right so. See you there around seven. Rathmore chapel. Might be smart to drive down tonight; it's farther than it appears on the map."

At the wine store, Donovan bought two bottles of Australian chardonnay and a bottle of McCallan's 18—his favorite single malt scotch.

Back in the Brennans' well-appointed kitchen, Sheila and Donovan cooked dinner and ate in an intimate little parlor, with a cozy fireplace, off the main dining room.

By the time they'd finished the salmon, a bottle and a half of the Australian chardonnay, most of the McCallan's, and said goodnight at the bottom of the stairs, they'd heard each other's life stories. Almost.

Donovan had heard about Sheila's career as a volunteer with *Médecins Sans Frontières*, her failed marriage to a French pediatrician she'd met in medical school, and her love of poetry, dance, and all sports, especially hiking and biking.

For his part, Donovan did not reveal his ordeal back in Killgarson or his mission in Rathmore. He didn't have to tell her about the kickboxing; like everyone else within miles, it seemed, she already had him pegged as a local legend.

He thought it only fair, however, to tell her about his three failed marriages, but not the details. She learned about his love of linguistics, of women in general, and his commitment to keeping his relationships platonic. She wondered why, and he said, "It just seems to work out better that way. They last longer. I got tired of losing good friends to moonlight and roses." She smiled and let it go.

It was eight hours after their first glass of McCallan's—3:00 a.m.—when they decided to call it a night. They embraced for a long time at the bottom of the stairs, she standing one step above so she was almost at his height. Finally, they stepped back, holding hands, gently letting go, reluctantly, without a word. Just long, soulful eye contact as she backed up the stairs. She threw him a kiss from the landing and flashed her gap-toothed smile before turning away.

Climbing the stairs to the third floor and closing his bedroom door, aware of her presence one floor down, Donovan was filled with that familiar rush of desire—aching, surging, visceral longing, in multiple shades of orange and red. There was no getting around that familiar feeling; perhaps he'd revisit that locked room again, after all.

Maybe it was the McCallan's, he mused, as he climbed into the cold, single bed. Maybe in the sober, gray light of morning, it would all evaporate. Maybe she'd be all business, focused on her bike tour, tonight a romantic fantasy in his single-malted imagination. Whatever it was, it would have to wait till after *the confession*, now just hours away. He set the alarm on his smartphone for 5:30 a.m. and was instantly asleep.

Donovan woke—a minute later, it seemed—to the voice of his favorite Irish poet, Conrad Fitzduff, asking why we bother getting up in the morning. He smiled at the alarm clock voice, poked the blinking phone off, and was on the road to Rathmore after a few cursory ablutions. No breakfast. Better to fast for the task at hand; he'd have a clearer head.

Arriving in the village, this time he parked some distance from the chapel, counting on a brisk walk to shake the hangover, get the blood flowing, and rehearse the plan one more time. He entered the chapel at exactly 6:30 a.m., aware that he'd be the only one present. The Sisters—ten aging nuns from the Our Lady of Lourdes Convent in Rathmore—would not be there until 7:00, the scheduled time for the morning Mass.

Donovan stepped into the confessional, knelt on the cushioned pad, and recalled the last time he'd been to confession. It had been in Killgarson, with Father McKenzie, the day he'd told him about the knife and being a fence. That's how it all began. Now, this is where it would all end, once the crooked places were set straight.

McKenzie breezed in, a few minutes late, his green vestments on, robe shining in the morning light as he pulled back the screen to allow that small window of access to the penitent. Donovan immediately went into the ritual so well ingrained.

"Bless me Father, for I have sinned."

McKenzie crossed himself, saying out loud, "In the name of the Father and of the Son and of the Holy Spirit. How long since your last confession?"

"Twenty-five years."

"Oh, my! You must have a lot to confess after all this time. But glad to see you've come back to the fold. What do you have to confess, my son?"

"I allowed my rapist to go free for twenty-five years without ever reporting him."

McKenzie drew a sharp breath, pausing, before continuing. "And did you participate in this sin in any willful way?"

"No, Father. I was assaulted and forced to submit, but I should have told my mother at the time. I was ashamed and afraid, but I now know that I was wrong not to. That's my fault. I committed a mortal sin by not having the courage to report this molester, but now I plan on making things right, beginning with this confession."

"What do you intend to do, my son?

"Well, Father, to begin with, I decided to allow the molester a chance to repent so that I wouldn't have to kill him. He wasn't worth the sacrifice of my own life, too. I have it all worked out; it's called a rite of passage."

"Is that all, my son?"

"There is one other thing, Father. I'd like you to listen to something you may find interesting."

Donovan poked the blinking face of his smartphone application, marked "Voice recorder: 0007," and the stern, high-pitched voice of Des McKenzie began: *"It struck me as high time you learned your lesson, one you wouldn't forget. The whiners may call it rape; we called it a rite of passage. I'd seen these rites of passage work fine in Africa. As I told you at the time, the elders found it made men out of those boys. Thought I'd do you a favor as a fatherless boy, help you grow up in a hurry. I must admit, the water treatment was my own idea."*

Donovan stopped the recorder and slid it back in his pocket before speaking.

"Thought you might want to hear what my molester sounded like before you give me absolution and a penance." Donovan said this in an even tone of voice, loud enough for anyone in the chapel outside to hear.

McKenzie, flushed with anger and confusion, gave up all pretense at hearing the confession. "Look, Mr. Donovan, I think it's time this little charade came to a close. There will be no absolution or penance. I have no idea what you think you're up to, but if you think blackmail is going to work here…"

"No, no, Des, you have it all wrong. I know it's not up to me to grant you absolution. That's way above my pay grade. What I can do is grant you forgiveness…for stealing my childhood and making me ashamed and panic-stricken for twenty-five years. I forgive you, and more importantly, I forgive myself for whatever part I may have played as victim or whiner. I thank you for pointing that out, really.

"Our talk last night was inspirational," Donovan continued. "I'm here this morning to bring you a gift, a rite of passage, one I think you'll find immensely beneficial, if somewhat difficult at first. I will promise not to give this tape to my reporter friend from *The Irish Times*—who is sitting in the chapel at this moment waiting for what I told him would be breaking news. Instead, I will give you a chance to redeem yourself in the eyes of God and in the eyes of the parish. 'Then you will know the truth, and the truth will set you free.' Isn't that the word of God that we all accept?"

McKenzie, suddenly aware that he might have walked into a trap, lowered his voice to a whispering hiss. "How do you suggest I do this? Walk out there and tell these old biddies I had relations with you twenty-five years ago? You must be mad."

"No, I'm honestly trying to give you the benefit of the doubt," Donovan said. "'Assume the best' is my policy. But first, I want to hear *your* confession, as a kind of dress rehearsal. Then I want you to do it for real, in public, before a nice, intimate gathering here in Rathmore. Trust me; as I said, I have it all worked out."

McKenzie, sweating profusely, wiping his brow with a handkerchief, was growing increasingly irate. "Listen, Donovan, if you think you can come in here and intimidate me like this, you have another thing coming. People here trust me, with good reason. Who's going to believe some violent, kickboxing Yank?"

Donovan smiled. "That may be true at the moment. But by the time we're through here, the world will know who I really am, and more importantly, who you really are, Des."

McKenzie wiped the sweat from his face, looked at Donovan holding the fear of a cornered animal in his eyes, and decided on a change of tactics.

"Look, Billy, it's not going to do any good to bring this kind of disgrace to this village. You may think it's just going to hurt me, but you're going to hurt a lot of innocent people who deserve better. Think of all those boys and their parents. Are you sure you want to do this?"

Donovan laughed out loud. "Wow! Suddenly a concern for the boys and their parents. Des, you are really a piece of work."

McKenzie leaned forward, his hands pressed together in a prayerful gesture. "Please, Billy, you don't want to do this. I have my flaws, I admit it, but this caper is just going to get you arrested. Let us just both walk away from this, and I promise not to press any charges."

"Too late!" Donovan declared, almost shouting, then lowered his voice. "I've set too many wheels in motion already. I don't think you want to read the headlines in the *Irish Times* tomorrow, with your picture under large print that says: 'Father Desmond McKenzie, Accused Pedophile in Rathmore, Denies Allegations.' Surely you don't want to join the whiners by claiming you were a victim."

"For God's sake, man, will you keep your voice down?" McKenzie pleaded. "I'll be a laughingstock in this village; they'd never understand. What do you want me to do? This is ridiculous."

"As I just said, I want to hear your confession, so that I know you have a clear conscience. Then I want you to follow a few simple instructions that will put all this behind us, where you'll take full responsibility for your actions and we can all move on. Neither whiners nor victims. Just mortal men seeking grace and redemption."

"All right, all right," McKenzie conceded, "I don't see that I have a choice. This is blackmail, so don't give me any of this clap-trap about grace and redemption. You'll burn in hell for this."

Donovan leaned closer to McKenzie and said, "I can see this is difficult for you, Des, but you'll feel better afterwards.

We always do once we've completed a rite of passage, hard as it might appear at the time. Here's the thing I want you to understand: I'm determined to give us *both* a chance for a new beginning. I was going to kill you; I even bought a gun. And you know something? I know that God would have forgiven me, as a matter of justice. Because if anyone ever deserved to die, it's you, Des. But seeing you yesterday inspired me to show mercy, to give you a chance, and not to have you die unrepentant, with all those crimes on your conscience."

"Can we get on with this?" McKenzie said. "I have a mass to conduct in a few minutes."

"It should be easy, Des," Donovan said. "All we need is the truth of what happened on that May morning in '77, nothing more or less. No need for embellishments."

Donovan set up the Canon 550 with the video cam focused on McKenzie's sweating face, and whispered: "I hope you don't mind if I record this. It's something posterity will find invaluable, don't you agree?" McKenzie said nothing, just bowed his head and crossed himself.

"Des," Donovan said emphatically, "I will now hear your confession. Kneel down and take it from the top."

McKenzie knelt obediently, pressed his cross to his sweaty lips, and began.

"Bless me, Lord, for I have sinned."

Donovan crossed himself and began the ritual: "In the name of the Father, and of the Son, and of the Holy Spirit. How long since your last confession?"

"Ten years."

"You must have a lot on your conscience."

"I do. I'm guilty of sodomy, assault, and violation of my celibacy vows over many years and on multiple occasions."

"Can you be more specific? How many years? How many occasions?"

"Thirty years. Dozens of occasions, too many to recall."

"An estimate will do. Roughly how many?"

"At least twenty-five, maybe more. I lost count. Most were the altar boys over the years and a few other consensual partners in the seminary, and with a lover in Africa."

"Anything else?"

"No."

"Do you repent your sins and vow to turn away from them in the future? Say it, Des!"

"Yes. I'm truly sorry for all the harm I've caused. I've been an evil person. I'm sorry…as God is my witness."

"Now for your penance."

"No!" McKenzie shouted, momentarily forgetting himself. Lowering his voice, he said, "You must be mad if you think I'm going to accept penance from some jumped-up Yank!"

Donovan ignored McKenzie's outburst, staying focused on the plan.

"For your penance, I want you to go out there and say Mass for the nuns, as usual. When it comes time to offer up the host, instead of the customary turning your back to the congregation, I want you to face them and confess your sins, as you've done to me.

"Here's what you'll say. I've written it for you so you don't have to worry about leaving anything out."

Donovan pushed a sheet of typed script toward the trembling hand of McKenzie, who took it and perused it briefly. "This is insane," McKenzie said, looking incredulous.

Donovan forged ahead, "After the speech, I want you to follow Archbishop Flaherty's example: Prostrate yourself on the altar, ask God's forgiveness, and pledge to resign and seek redemption in a life of service to be decided by your superiors in the Archdiocese."

McKenzie glanced at the speech, wiped the sweat from his brow again, and said, "There's no way I'm going to subject myself to this kind of humiliation. I'd rather die."

Donovan looked at the defiant, sweating face and felt the familiar rage well up. "Listen, Des. That could be arranged, and not in a manner you'd enjoy. Do you have any idea how close you are to pushing me beyond my limit? One more word of resistance, and kickboxing will see a massive resurgence right here in this chapel. I'm this close." Donovan held his thumb and index finger a hair apart in the grate before McKenzie's face.

For the first time, McKenzie's eyes lost their amphibian indifference and registered animal-like fear.

"All right, I'll do it," he blurted.

"You've made a wise decision, Father McKenzie," Donovan said quietly. "Go in peace and may the Lord be with you."

McKenzie gathered up his prayer book and stepped briskly toward the vestry to change his vestments and start the Mass.

Donovan crossed himself, shut off the Canon recorder, and slid the confession grid back in place before stepping into the dimly lit chapel. The sexton had lit the candles on the altar, and a handful of people were scattered around the pews in small clusters. The sexton, a wizened little man in his seventies, knelt in the back, alone.

Donovan strode past the nuns, spotted Declan McCann, his old college roommate, and noted the camera crew setting up by the side entrance.

Donovan and McCann shook hands and chatted briefly, Donovan nodding affirmatively. Yes, the trek down from Dublin would be worth the journalist's time, as he'd assured him in the phone call. Front page news tomorrow. Then Donovan went to the back of the chapel, dipped his hand in the granite holy water font, and crossed himself in a moment of reverence for the power of truth, however long denied. He sat, waiting for the Mass to begin, feeling tense, not trusting McKenzie to follow through. For a moment, he felt he might pass out from pure exhaustion.

Thirty minutes dragged by, and the congregation—though accustomed to waiting—had begun to glance around, getting restless. An older man in the back hobbled out; the nuns all sat up in their pews, reading their novenas.

At 7:45, the word came: there would be no Mass this morning. Not by Father McKenzie. Not today, not ever. A young, uniformed garda, who looked like a gangly teenager, delivered the news: "I'm sorry to be the bearer of this sad news," he began in a trembling voice, "but a terrible accident has happened out on the Dublin Road, involving Father McKenzie. Sergeant Byrne just called it into the station. Apparently, Father McKenzie's Austin Healy was pullin' out o' the JP filling station—the one past the Clane roundabout; he must've never seen the Volvo lorry comin'."

Speaking with the garda informally outside, Donovan learned that the tiny Austin Healy convertible had been crushed like a beer can, McKenzie's body mangled beyond recognition. The lorry driver had escaped with some minor bruises and was not charged.

People stood around in small groups outside the chapel, expressing their grief and outrage at the "speeding" lorry driver.

Questions came in spurts with few answers, but no shortage of speculation.

What had Father McKenzie been doing on the Dublin Road when he was supposed to be saying Mass? How could he not have seen the lorry? It was on a dry straightway, visible for half a mile. Why had he been going to Dublin so soon again? Hadn't he just come back? And why hadn't he told anyone he wouldn't be saying Mass if he'd had to leave in such a hurry?

Donovan didn't wait for the gossip-driven post-mortem. Declan McCann was waiting for him outside the chapel with an impatient look on his face.

"Hey, Billy, what gives? What am I supposed to make of this? I was hoping to hear the BIG NEWS you promised firsthand, but secondhand will do. What was Father McKenzie going to announce?"

"That's confidential, Declan," Donovan replied. "I'm not at liberty to say. I'm under oath not to divulge anything beyond what I've already told you. Besides, the accident and its surroundings should be news enough to hold your editor for one day."

Donovan moved to get in the Vauxhall, but McCann, flushed with anger, blocked his path, an insistent hand up in protest.

"Wait a feckin' minute, Billy! You entice me down here with a breathless tip about a news scoop—with me asking my editor to hold a full page for a guaranteed hot news feed tomorrow—and this is all you have to say? What d'ya take me for, a proper eejit? Well, I'll have a few things to write about you, you can bet your Yank's arse on that."

"Suit yourself, Declan. A man just died. And now you want me to betray his confidence before his corpse is even cold? I thought Irish journalists shared a taboo against ambulance chasing. Or is that just when you're in high dudgeon in your anti-American polemics?"

"So now we're a full-fledged Yank, is it? Looking down on the primitives. You've come a long way, Billy D., from an ignorant Killgarson culchie to a fucken Yank. I can't say I notice any improvement. Read all about it in the next edition."

They locked stares as they backed away, stepping into their respective cars at the same time without another word.

"Feck you, McCann," Donovan muttered, still angry and stunned. "Always was a bit of a gobshite. Always thought it was about the Great Declan McCann. No change there."

Donovan had one more call to make, this time in Kilkenny. He gunned the Astra onto the northbound road toward the walled city, looking forward to the familiar drive, and excited about what awaited him at the end of it.

He suddenly realized he was famished, blood sugar in his shoes. Glancing at his watch, he saw that if he was lucky, there was a chance he could still make the Craigmore Nursing Home in time to take his old friend to a late breakfast.

Donovan found Tommy Dixon in robust health, now in his eighties, powerful shoulders still square, gray curls overflowing onto his tweed collar. The only impairment he could detect was a slight deafness in Tommy's left ear, which Billy quickly accommodated with rearranged seats.

"Oh, God, Billy D., I'd know you anywhere," was Dixon's delighted opener.

"Tommy Dixon, you look like a million bucks," Donovan declared, as they shook hands. "What are they feeding you?" He smiled inwardly at the powerful grip of his old mentor, the huge hands still gnarled from the years of farm labor.

They went to breakfast at Mt. Juliet Hotel—an upscale restaurant, Donovan's treat. They talked for hours: of the great kickboxing champions and their moves, of the championships they'd won together, of the opponents, and of the legacy Tommy had bequeathed to Kilkenny.

Near the end of the conversation, Tommy brought them back to that June day in 1978, under the giant oak in Dixon's meadow—the day Billy D. found his deliverance lifeline.

"Ya know, Billy D., even before that, I always knew ya was special, even before the kickboxing. There was something about ya, as a young lad, the way ya carried yerself, the look in yer eye. I don't know how else to say it."

Looking at the beloved, wrinkled face, remembering what he owed this legend of a man, Donovan fought back the tears. He reached across the table, squeezed Tommy's hand, and said, "You know something, Tommy? Without you, I wouldn't be here. That's the truth. You literally saved my life. There's a place reserved in heaven for great souls like yours."

Tommy looked back at him, tears brimming over in the kind, blue eyes. Embarrassed, he coughed into his hand and muttered, "I'd better be getting back. They'll think I've skipped town up at the nursing home."

They drove to Craigmore in silence, content with the comfort of each other's presence, taking in the beauty of the picket-fence stud farms, the newborn thoroughbred foals racing in the clovered meadows—free as the wind whipping through their blonde manes.

Walking up the gravel path to the majestic nursing home, Tommy turned to Donovan and said, "Now don't be a stranger, Billy D.; ya know where to find me. Maybe we could talk you into giving a kickboxing exhibition down at the Dixon Center wan o' dese days."

"That's entirely possible, Tommy," Donovan replied. "But right now, I have to go see a girl about a bike tour. She promised me that all I'll have to do is pedal."

Tommy grinned. "I'm sure ye'll do a lot more than pedal, or yer not the Billy D. I know."

They beamed at each other, shook hands firmly, standing close, and parted—the heavy, brass-plated door of the nursing home closing solemnly behind the beloved head of gray curls.

Donovan paused in front of the closed door and smiled affectionately before getting back in the car.

Then, with a rush of excitement, he turned the Vauxhall south and gunned it down the winding road toward Glendunne House.

MASTER CARNEY'S CARD SCHOOL

MASTER CARNEY'S CARD SCHOOL

PERHAPS IT'S THE ISOLATION, OR the incessant rain and the all-too-familiar personalities; it might even be the insatiable appetite of human beings for novelty and stimulation. Whatever the reason, it is a universal rule of village life that people seem to favor the darkest interpretation of their neighbors' foibles—especially if they come steeped in webs of intrigue, in chains of unexplained events involving people of privilege, whose elevated pretensions are always a joy to see tumbling back to earth.

Imagine, then, the burst of excitement that stirred in the mischievous heart of our tiny village, Rathdargin, when, right in the middle of Sunday Mass, one of our most respected parishioners fell face-down, unconscious, draped across the chapel doorstep, having just knocked over the heavy, granite holy water font as he stumbled from his pew in the back row, spewing profanities in a slurred, stricken voice. This is about as good as it gets, from a gossipmonger's standpoint. And in Rathdargin, tongue-wagging was a village sport with practically no bystanders, all long-practiced in the art of embellishment and darkened relay.

It happened on a beautiful June morning, 1952. I was a ten-year-old altar boy, in my second year of serving Mass, having arrived early to set up for the service. On my way to the sacristy at the back of the chapel, I noticed several cars and a large lorry parked outside Master Carney's residence, which was just a short distance north of the chapel. This was a typical rural Irish village layout: church, school, schoolmaster's residence—all in a row, usually within handy walking distance of the pub and grocery store. In Rathdargin, the latter was P. J. Ryan's Pub—seat of passionate, fact-free, Guinness-fueled political debates, from the Battle of the Boyne (1690) to the Easter Rising (1916)—all discussed as if they were current affairs.

One curiosity this Sunday morning was the cluster of cars, and the big, wide-wheel lorry blocking half the road after being hastily parked and forgotten. Since the Master didn't own a car, and it was too early for any parishioners, the only other suspect was Father Gilligan, and he was not likely to show before nine twenty-nine, sweating and breathless, cutting it close—for the 9:30 Mass. So who owned all these vehicles? I wondered.

I didn't linger on it at the time—too busy setting up for Mass; I just shrugged and assumed that Master Carney must have a lot of family visiting from Mayo, his home county in Connemara, on the west coast of Ireland.

The Master was an anomaly in Rathdargin, a remote speck of a village in southeast Leinster province. As one of his students who'd quit school before my thirteenth birthday, I wrote a detailed rendering of his teaching persona—with the benefit of long distance hindsight—in a coming-of-age memoir set in this community in the post-WWII era:[1]

Laim J.Carney, B.A., M.Phil., Ph.D., walks in with a no-nonsense stride. He is wearing a once-expensive, rumpled, shiny, blue serge suit.

---

1 *Far from the Land: An Irish Memoir* (2009).

His shirt, too, is stained and rumpled, though he has a clean, detach-able white collar that clashes with the shabby shirt. His tie is a syn-thetic clip-on of indescribable shades of green and yellow. To the casual observer, it would appear that here is an unkempt character, indifferent to style or fashion. Until you see his shoes, which instantly clash with this assumption: They're a fine pair of black Italian imports with an elegant shine—a vestigial symbol of social status seldom found in villages like Rathdargin.

Carney is about forty-five years old, six feet tall, broad-shouldered and ruggedly handsome. His mouth has a slightly cruel twist—which can be mocking and cynical, or charming, depending on the mood or the target of his slashing rhetoric. The Master's full head of graying hair and well-bred eyes give him an aura of sophistication that, like the shoes, immediately clashes with the schoolhouse and its bedraggled pupils. He's a dead ringer for Richard Burton, the famous actor, and passersby often mistake him for Burton on the streets of Dublin—seeking his autograph and wanting to have their photos snapped with him.

But Carney was no Richard Burton, if by that we mean a man of refinement and class. Halfway past the fireplace on his way to the podium, this fountain of knowledge and teacher of youth clears his throat and spits profusely on the dusty, decaying floor. He slides his polished shoe across the phlegm, as though killing some vile crustacean. The pupils stare straight ahead, pretending not to notice the vulgarity, though one girl in the fifth row fails to muffle a nervous giggle.

This was Master Liam Carney in a nutshell, a man of elite education and rare intellect who, after years of boredom in the isolated rural schoolhouse, had become an alcoholic and a manipulative derelict. I'd been his "teacher's assistant" before I dropped out, tired of covering for him as a substitute teacher while he indulged his addiction at P. J. Ryan's Pub. He got started early each morning—right after roll call, the only task he bothered to complete on any given day—because it was the only thing he was held accountable for by the Irish Free State.

One of the things that always amazed just about everyone in the village was how Carney could "hold his liquor." Here was a man who could start at P. J. Ryan's around 10:00 in the morning, drink till closing time at 10:00 p.m., retire to another drinking session at his "Residence"— the teachers' free bungalow adjoining the school—with his hard-core drinking and gambling (cards) buddies, and still carry on a perfectly coherent, well-informed conversation on a wide array of subjects. Not that he was particularly admired for this; it merely added another layer of intrigue to the enigmatic Master Liam Carney.

That lovely June morning, the Mass started on time, and, as usual, I was preoccupied with my part in the order of service, my back to the packed-in congregation. Shortly after the opening prayer, I heard the crash. It would have been impossible to miss, since it felt as if a small earthquake had erupted in the back of the chapel. The first sound was a crunching thud of granite against concrete, sending a tremor all the way up the rugged tile floor to where we knelt on the altar steps. Next came a series of hoarse profanities, slurred and unclear, but loud enough to make us blush as altar boys—knowing the curses were at least venial sins, probably mortal since uttered in God's house. Finally, on the heels of the string of oaths, came a second sound: a soft plop; then, silence.

Everyone remained frozen for several seconds, all wondering what to do. After what seemed like hours, as if on some invisible command, the congregation rushed as one to the back of the chapel, eager to be the first eyewitness to…God knows what. I started to charge down there, too, with my fellow members of the "angel corps," when I caught Father Gilligan's glare. "Sit down and be quiet!" he hissed. "No need to join the mob." We sat as told, of course, while the priest strolled slowly down the aisle, parting the crowd by the door, then ushered everyone back to their pews so that we might proceed with the Mass, which had been so rudely interrupted.

Father Gilligan made no mention of the event in the service that morning, nor ever again, as far as I know.

What I do know is that Jackie Quinn quickly became the center of attention in the village. For it was Jackie who was found unconscious on the chapel steps and had to be rushed to St. Vincent's Emergency Room in Carlow, twenty miles away, where he was treated and released a few days later. This was where the craic (fun) began, for no credible explanation was ever offered by Jackie or his family beyond the muttered comment that he "didn't feel so well" that morning. Henry Ford could not have designed a more reliable engine to fan the flames of speculation, which would expand in proportion to the most fertile imaginations in the village for years to come.

What made it all the more juicy was the character at the center of the event. Jackie Quinn was the second oldest of a highly respected farm family in nearby Knockmore. He was handsome, with a strong build, but not big; about five ten, with wavy auburn hair. He was a good football player, determined and unassuming, who'd drink a pint with the boys—though often alone—in O'Connors's Pub in Borris after a game. Unlike many young men in his hard-drinking crowd, he was never known to be drunk or rowdy. Quite the contrary: He was consummately polite, soft-spoken, and gifted with a droll wit that had people laughing and relaxed in his presence.

Jackie had emigrated to England for a brief stint, but like many Irish laborers from large farms, soon gave up the adventure and came home to work on the family farm. During the slower times on the farm—between spring planting and harvest in the fall—he would sometimes drive a truck for T. R. ("Ter") Neill & Sons, local jobber and entrepreneur in Borris—our largest village. Ter Neill contracted long distance hauling of coal, livestock feed, and lumber. His routes usually involved a drive to Dublin, sixty miles north of Carlow, but given the primitive roads and stop-and-go conditions in small towns, the usual drive was an eight-hour trip, often pushing the day to twelve hours or more—with the driver arriving home after midnight, exhausted and famished. This was Jackie's standard routine in 1952, and the backdrop to the mysterious collapse in the chapel that Sunday morning.

I left Ireland in 1959—seven years after the incident—and, as was true with dozens of other local mysteries, The Case of Jackie Quinn remained unsolved. In fact, I never gave it a second thought until I was back home on vacation some ten years later and stopped into O'Connor's Pub in the center of town. I was not there to drink, but to buy my Uncle Peter his favorite whiskey, Jameson, before driving the final three miles to their farm in Ballybrack, my mother's ancestral home. Who should be sitting at the bar—in his customary spot with his lone pint of Guinness—but Jackie Quinn? The mystery man himself. He turned to face me when I walked in, smiled his gentle half smile, and greeted me quietly with, "Oh, God, Myles, is that you? Sure I never thought I'd live to see you in these parts again. Let me buy ya a drink."

That was pure Jackie Quinn—making every returning emigrant feel as if he were a long-lost friend. I immediately flashed back to the altar that Sunday morning, almost two decades earlier, but before I could pursue it, several old friends and neighbors spotted me. Soon, a festive atmosphere prevailed in the pub—helped by several lavish rounds of Guinness and shots of Jameson.

After the first gush of welcomes and inquiries about my mother and sisters, I steered the conversation toward my long-standing curiosity: "What happened that Sunday morning in the chapel, Jackie? I've always wondered about the real story there. Would you mind telling? After all, it's been seventeen years!"

O'Connor's Pub was jumping at this point. I'd drawn a crowd as the returning Yank, and now there was an opportunity to revisit history—a shared passion—and hear yet another rendition from the horse's mouth. Jackie took a sip of his Guinness, cleared his throat—signaling he was ready to launch—and the crowd settled in for yet another version of the famous story.

"Sure, I don't mind atall," Jackie declared, trying to get Jimmy O'Connor's attention, stalling with practiced nonchalance. "What are ya drinkin' dere, Myles? Jimmy, give dis man his favorite drink. No bether man ever left Borris. A great football player! Ah, Jaysus, Myles, it's grand ta see ya. Ya remind me of all da good auld times we had back in dose days—long gone now. But sure it was great craic all da same..."

"Thanks, Jackie," I replied hastily, ignoring the pints and shots already stacking up on the bar from well-wishers. "I'll just have a mineral, if you don't mind. I have to drive back to Dublin tonight. But tell me about the accident before we forget. I'm dying to know what happened. I was just an altar boy at the time, and no one would tell me anything. It was a BIG mystery."

Finally, Jackie had what he needed: everyone's attention.

"Right so. Well, Myles, ya remember Master Carney, God rest his soul—died o' lung cancer a couple o' years back, poor auld divil. Anyway, The Master had dis regular card game at 'The Residence' every Saturday night. I'd been drivin' for Ter Neill an da Dublin run—haulin' coal, an' wire, an' anyt'ing else we needed down here. Since I always got home late, they'd be starvin', an' sure Carney never asked anyone if dey had a mouth an 'im till I showed up wid da mate. I'd bring about twelve big pork chops from Bill Breen's in Naas—great big chunks o' mate dat ya couldn't get from Dillon or Nowlan here in Borris..."

Worried that he was off on a tangent, I interrupted: "You're right about that, Jackie, but what did pork chops have to do with what happened in the chapel?"

"Bear wid me," Jackie said, hand on my arm, "I'm getting ta dat. As ye'll see, it had a lot ta do wid it. Where was I? Oh, right, I was talkin' about bringin' da mate ta Carney's card game. I gets back ta Rathdargin around midnight—maybe a little after—fecked from twelve hours an da road. I have da pork chops, da usual standin' order from Carney's card school, which was an all-night affair, every Saturday night, in da normal course o' events."

"Don't forget about the Brylcreem," Bill Doyle, a neighbor, warned, with a wink.

"Sure, I was getting' ta dat part," Jackie said, patiently, taking time to light another Player cigarette off the butt in his hand.

"After quenchin' de thirst wid a quick pint," he continued, "Carney digs out de fryin' pan an asks me for da lard. What lard? Sez I. De lard I ordered, sez he. I never remember any lard bein' ordered, sez I. Right, sez he. And da next t'ing I know Carney darts upstairs an' comes down wid a big jar o' Brylcreem, like Bill just said—ya remember dat auld white, greasy stuff, Myles?"

I nodded, remembering how The Master always smelled of the pungent hair oil. "Don't tell me he was already gearing up to go to Mass."

"No, no…dis had nuthin' ta do wid Mass. He had somethin' else in mind altogether, 'n' ya'd never guess what. Myles, I'll buy a round for the whole pub if ya can guess what comes next."

Mick Murphy, Bill McGee, Jim Flood—all former neighbors of mine—and all the rest of the jam-packed pub, were all leaning in now, listening intently to Jackie's story, already knowing the punch line from hearing it dozens of times, enjoying their advantage and my stumped reaction.

"I give up," I said, "I have no idea what Carney might have done next."

"Of course ya don't," Jackie agreed, with his trademark smile. "Dat's why they called him The Master. He was, in his own way. Carney takes a spoon an' scoops out a few huge dollops o' da Brylcreem an' slaps it on da pan dat's already smokin' on da auld Aga stove. He throws in a few onions, t'en da pork chops, an' da smoke n' smell o' da pork cookin' in hair oil nearly drove us all outa da kitchen. Carney's acting like he's goin' for Chef o' da Year, chain smoking his Players an' dealin' cards without missin' a trick. I asked for another drink an' dat's whin da disaster dawned: we were outa Guinness, dry as a bone, an' no place ta go until P. J. Ryans's Pub opened after Mass. At three in da mornin', dis is serious business, Myles. It's an absolute, total fucken disaster."

Jackie paused to sip his pint and light another Player off the half one in his hand, looking choked up at the horror of the memory. The pub crowd waited, cradling their pints, knowing what was coming next, yet hanging on every word.

"Don't forget about da methylated spirits," Jim Flood chimed in.

"Sure, I'm getting ta dat," Jackie repeated, waving Flood off with a cloud of Player smoke.

"Like I was saying," Jackie continued, giving the others a sly look, "Carney is only getting started; he stays calm an' upbeat while we're all panickin'. He serves up da pork chops an' we're all so famished by now dat da Brylcreem no longer matters. T'en he sez, 'I have a treat for you gentlemen, at least for those of you man enough to join me in a little experiment in chemistry.' Wid dat, he lights up a couple o' candles, shuts down da Tilly Lamp on da kitchen table, an' pours out five shots o' warm methylated spirits—Myles, remember that clear, blue liquid dat fueled da Tilly Lamps?—directly from da lamp, wid all dat crud floatin' around. I think it was some kind of pure, uncut alcohol; deadly stuff, no smell. Could kill an ox."

"Dat's the God's honest truth," Tony Cosgrave attested. "Sure poor auld Mickey Davitt went stone blind after drinking just wan shot o' the stuff up at a huntin' lodge in Wexford. An' two of his cousins died the same night."

Several other drinkers clamored to attest to their memory of the blue liquid and its lethal qualities. Jackie took another deep draught of the Guinness, acknowledging the testimonial givers, before continuing.

"At dis point, we were all so far gone we couldn't o' cared less. I didn't even ask about poisonin', since Carney was an educated man an' wasn't about ta poison himself an' da rest of us. Or at least dat's what I thought at da time, if I thought atall. We all downed our shots together, an' I swear ta God, I've never had liquor burn me throat like dat—all the way down. I felt like I was on fire. We all did. We staggered around, grabbing our throats, screamin' in agony. We downed several pints o' water, got some relief, den fell on da pork chops like dere was no tomorrow. The Master was unfazed; he just dealt another hand o' cards, askin' us if we'd anted up.

"As God is me witness," Jackie declared, "I don't remember a t'ing after dat until I'm kneelin' in da chapel. I have no idea how I got ta Mass, but I do remember lookin' up, an' dere's Father Gilligan liftin' da chalice up toward da heavens. Next t'ing I know, da priest—in green vestments wid a big, yellow dove on his back—is risin' up from da altar, headin' for da rafters, like Christ risen from da tomb. I'm kneelin' dere in da back pew wid da prime boys, barely hangin' on. T'en Carney marches in, all decked out, an strides right up ta his usual pew in da front o' da chapel, fresh as a daisy, like he'd had a good night's rest.

"Dat's whin it struck me dat Father Gilligan couldn't be risin' up like dat. It had ta be me, Myles, and that's whin I put two 'n' two together—da methylated spirits, da pork chops, da Brylcreem—dey couldn't have been good for me, right? D'ya see what I'm sayin?"

"Absolutely, Jackie. I see your reasoning there," I assured him earnestly.

The others nodded solemnly, too, as though we'd cracked some esoteric puzzle that few in the universe were clever enough to master. The feeling in the pub was one of exquisite camaraderie.

Jackie lit another Player, took a deep drag, and paused for a lengthy exhale before going for the *pièce de résistance*, seemingly with perfect recall: "I make for da chapel door, but before I can get out, da whole buildin' starts spinnin' out o' control. I reach for da holy water font to steady meself, an' da next t'ing I know, I wake up wid a lovely nurse leanin' over me in da hospital ward saying, 'Yer awake, Mr. Quinn. Thought we were going to lose you there for a while. Try to stay away from those methylated spirits next time.'

"I looked at her," Jackie said, looking serene, "so young, so innocent, an' thought of Liam Carney, Player in hand, an' dat night in The Residence. She didn't hafta worry. I wouldn't be back for Carney's Saturday night card school if ya said one t'ousand Masses for me. No more pork chops from Bill Breen's butcher shop. Ever since, I've had nothin' but a pint o' Guinness. It's hard to get in much trouble, Myles, if you just stick ta da Guinness."

I said goodnight to all my old friends, tore myself loose from their gnarled handshakes and hard back thumps, thanked Jackie for clearing up the mystery, paid O'Connor for the Jameson, and made for the door, happy to be home, basking in the knowledge that this village had produced so much talent, gifted in so many fields: poetry, athletics, music, singing, dancing, storytelling, and teaching.

In the case of my old teacher, Master Liam Carney, his unmistakable genius would forever redound, not on teaching, but on two darker art forms: deviance and debauchery. In those unheralded, more exacting forms, there might be other contenders—amateurs and wannabes—but there would be only one true giant, towering above all in creativity, consistency, and commitment—worthy of being called The Master.

It was a privilege to have known him so well.

DREAMS OF TRAMORE

DREAMS OF TRAMORE

WHEN MOTHER FIRST MADE THE announcement, we thought we'd finally driven her around the bend.

The night had begun as usual, no inkling of any drama afoot. We'd all been milling around the kitchen after supper, arguing over chores—an art form we'd perfected—my five older sisters, Mother, and me, the youngest and only boy. The sisterhood ranged in age from thirteen to eighteen, and I'd just turned nine.

It was April of 1950, and Mother was raising us alone—Da had long since abandoned the family—on an isolated, rocky piece of land in the foothills of Mt. Leinster, Ireland. Three years earlier, she'd somehow managed to keep the seven of us alive during "The Blizzard of '47," which had dropped fifteen feet of snow on the entire island one February night, killing a third of the island's population and most of the livestock.

I can still see her black coat with the muslin sack sticking out of the pocket, as she dug her way through the massive drifts, disappearing around the bend in the laneway. She did that every day for two months, returning at nightfall with a sack of potatoes from a neighboring farm—the difference between life and death that interminable winter.

That struggle for survival made a lasting impact, so much so that "47" was never far from our minds. We never quite recovered from the trauma of losing all the livestock—a flock of thirty sheep, two ponies, and two cows. It's anybody's guess how Mother made ends meet. It was certainly without help from Da; he never even wrote, let alone sent money or a word of encouragement.

As children, we'd taken for granted what Mother called our "hand-to-mouth" existence, and it was only from magazines and visits to their friends' houses that the sisterhood began to chafe at the scarcity and hardship that now began to feel unjust and humiliating to their lofty teenage pride.

Our sole respite from this seething undercurrent was a nightly fantasy game that launched us into a parallel universe. Every child could play, and did. All we needed was an opener—usually my role—and the rest flowed like a mountain stream.

"Where are we going for summer holidays this year?" I asked casually, though we'd never been on holidays anywhere.

"Let's go to Dublin and go shopping on Grafton Street," my sister Tess gushed, in her best Hollywood persona, one befitting her standing as the blonde femme fatale of the family. "I'll buy a fur coat and a pearl necklace at Arnotts."

"Yeah, and on the way, let's buy a limousine and stop by the circus in New Ross," Rosie, our natural comedian, added with a straight face.

"Wait! Don't forget the giraffes," Noreen volunteered, always the animal lover.

"No, I want to see the lions," I argued, just to say something.

At that point, Bernadette ("Bernie"), our alpha sister with the romantic soul, had heard enough.

"This is all rubbish," she proclaimed, standing in the middle of the kitchen floor. "We're not gonna waste time at any crummy circus in New Ross; we're goin' ta buy a big red bus—a double decker like they have in Dublin—an' go straight ta Butler's restaurant in Kilkenny, the one with waiters in tuxedos, an' we're gonna have a seven course meal—champagne toast to start, then soup, steak and roast potatoes with creamed cauliflower and Brussels sprouts, trifle for dessert, cheese and crackers, Irish coffee, then brandy and cigars all around. Then we'll all go waltzing at the Ritz and dance until dawn."

She'd been reading the British tabloids again about the lifestyles of English lords and ladies living in Irish castles.

Biding my time till Bernie had exhausted everyone, I played my favorite ace: "I don't care about all that other stuff; I want ta go ta de carnival in Tramore, drive me own bumpin' car, then have fish n' chips an' soft-serve ice cream on the Strand."

I knew this was a surefire winner that the sisterhood would let me have, giving rise to another round of outlandish fantasies, for even in this crowded field of bottomless yearnings, we all knew that one in particular rose up like an Everest, trumping all contenders with that ecstatic, magical word: *TRAMORE.*

Though just past Kilkenny over the Blackstairs Range in neighboring County Waterford, Tramore might as well have been on another planet, a heavenly planet laden with a bountiful array of all the longed-for things we'd dreamed about. Any member of the Hogan family—including Mother—could have told you of Tramore's wonders without missing a beat.

Bernie took the bait right off. "Billy's right, ya know! Where else are we gonna find one of the greatest seaside resorts in the world, where ya can see all the way ta Wales on a clear day? We can still have our seven course dinner an' go waltzing, too."

"That's right," Tess agreed, to our collective amazement— since those two never agreed on anything. "I hear it has everything: circus, carnival, merry-go-round, fish and chips, and all the lemonade ya can drink. An' waltzing as well."

Bernie could never stand anyone agreeing with her, especially her younger sister.

"Who d'ya t'ink yer kiddin?" she asked, as if confronting some arch villain. "We know da real reason ya want ta go ta Tramore is because o' Metal Man. It's always de same with you, Tess Hogan—yer just mad ta find a man, any man, even if he's a lump o' iron."

"Look who's talkin'," Tess fired back. "What are ya planning on waltzing with in Kilkenny—a woman? An' whose always goin' on about romantic dinners an' moonlight serenades. Now who's really man-mad, Bernie Hogan?" They always used each other's last name as a put-down, one of the many things about the sisterhood I never understood.

"All right, all right, you two," Mother interrupted wearily. "Yer about ta give me a headache. We're supposed to be having fun, remember?"

I stopped listening to their squabbling, as the sisterhood now outdid each other with the endless delights of Tramore: stalls where you won big prizes just for throwing a ball or winning a raffle; candy stores the size of small fields; crates of chocolate éclairs, toffee, and licorice; and, most important of all, soft-serve ice cream stands with *both* vanilla and chocolate.

Tess and Bernie were still yapping at each other when Mother stood up, pulled back her chair, and waved her arms for attention.

"Hush up, Bernie! Tess!" she said firmly, looking around the kitchen to be sure we were all there. "Now listen everyone, I have some good news. Is everyone here? Right so…This is it: I've decided that this is the summer we're actually going to Tramore.

You've all been good children, and I've saved up enough, so we're going. I think we all need a good day out, away from the farm and chores. What do ya think?"

She beamed in her best smile, expecting us to be thrilled. Instead, we just stared at her in stunned disbelief.

Finally, Tess broke the awkward silence: "Mammy, yer joking, right?" Tess stammered, suddenly short of breath. "Don't joke about this. I think I'm goin' ta faint. Jesus, Mary, and Joseph, please make this come true."

"Oh, it's going to come true all right," Mother said, her eyes determined. "I've already booked the van and made arrangements with Tommy Leach to milk the Kerry cow that day. It's all set."

Suddenly, as if on some invisible signal, we all started yelling and screaming, jumping around the kitchen floor, piling on each other gleefully, like puppies.

Instantly, we had a million questions: When are we going? How will we get there? Who else will be there? Why did we have to wait till now? Why not before now? For how long?

Mother had thought it all through, of course. She was like that. "I've booked Jimmy Murphy for August tenth, she said, looking worried. "We'll leave early that morning and come home after supper. It'll be a great day out at the beach and carnival."

"Does this mean we'll have supper in Tramore?" Noreen asked, in her quiet way.

"Yes, we can have fish and chips, with Corcoran's lemonade," Mother assured us. "As long as you all behave yourselves."

Fish and chips was the ultimate delicacy, and we only got lemonade once a year at the August fifteenth Mass—known as the "patron"—held at the ancestors' graveyard in Rathdargan, our communal Memorial Day.

August was the height of the tourist season, so Mother had obviously done some planning, since Jimmy Murphy was the only taxi in Rathdargan. We would travel in style in his Green Vauxhall van, our chariot to Paradise.

When the first blush of excitement wore off, I began to worry about how Mother was going to pay for all this. Being the youngest, and the only son, I was privy to more of Mother's money problems than any member of the sisterhood. From the time I could talk, she'd always treated me as her confidant, not wanting "to bother the girls," as she put it.

"Sure, there's no use in worrying them," she'd say. "They'll have their own grown-up problems soon enough without having to worry about mine."

I sometimes wondered why she told me so much, but I was particularly worried about Tramore, since she'd always told me we could never afford to go to there.

"Why not, Mammie?" I'd pressed. "It's just a beach!"

"Well, everything there costs wads of money," she'd answered, looking tired and sad. "It's not just a beach, son. It's what's called a resort, an' ya need a fashionable bathing suit an' nice clothes. Only rich people can afford ta go there. They stay in the swanky hotels, drink cocktails on the balcony, an' wear fancy dinner gowns and expensive jewelry. In the afternoon, they stroll on the promenade, sometimes with little pet dogs on leashes. Some even have maids to walk the dogs. It's not our kinda place. They're not our kinda people."

"How d'ya know about all dese t'ings, Mammie?" I'd asked. "Were ya ever dere, in Tramore?"

"No, son, I could never afford it," she'd replied. "But I worked as a parlor maid for a wealthy English family before I got married. They vacationed at lots of fancy places, like the French Riviera and exclusive Italian resorts in the Mediterranean. Places like Tramore."

That settled it for me, as it did for the sisterhood. We'd all loved the glittering images of those exotic places, but never doubted that they were out of our reach—as was everything, it seemed, beyond our farm's boundaries.

Up to now, we'd had great sport outdoing each other with fantasies of the mythical Tramore. But now that we were actually going there, the game shifted from who had the most fertile imagination to whose imagination was going to be indulged first.

That's where Bernie's Metal Man jab came in.

His history had a tragedy at its center. In 1816, a British military transport ship named Sea Horse, carrying a naval battalion and many of their families, ran aground and wrecked in Tramore Bay—a treacherous body of water that was easily mistaken by ships at sea for a safe haven in the Waterford estuary. The shipwreck claimed the lives of everyone aboard: 292 men and 71 women and children.

To prevent a recurrence, Lloyds of London funded the construction of three gigantic piers to warn sailors of the danger. One of the piers featured a massive, cast-iron sentry pointing seaward, warning seafarers of the dangerous shallows.

The statue was famously known as "Metal Man"—and he had a rich store of myths and legends deriving from his pedigree. The most popular of these myths was that if a single woman could hop barefoot around the base of Metal Man three times, she'd be married within the year.

This had the same mythic potency as hearing the wail of the banshee (harbinger of a death in the family) or seeing a rainbow's end on your land (marking the location of a pot of gold).

No one with an ounce of Celtic blood doubted the veracity of these beliefs.

Leading up to August tenth, testimonials piled up regarding Metal Man's prowess as a matchmaker, as our nightly "ramblers"—drop-ins from the neighborhood—revisited romantic histories.

"It's a fact," Mick Murphy announced, "dat Mary Doran met Billy Larkin only three weeks after her first hop, back in 1933. He proposed six months later."

Jim Breen told a story I didn't understand, but it made everyone laugh: "Shiela Roach had been engaged to George Scully for *fourteen years* until she hopped around Metal Man wan summer. An' guess what? They *had ta* get married four months later. Tell me that was a coincidence! No feckin' way."

"Oh, sure now," Jack Brennan confessed, "me own Ma—she was Mary Doyle as a girl—swears that she'd never have landed da auld fella, a confirmed bachelor over on Skellig Mountain, had it not been for Metal Man. An' she was not one ta gild the lily, I'll tell ya. Dere's got to be somet'in' to it."

"Well, there may be somethin' to it," Mother announced abruptly. "But I have to get up at five in the mornin', Metal Man, match-maker or not, so I'd like yez all to get up an' go home now."

The ramblers were used to this from Mother, so they cheerfully obliged, taking their time, chatting about other conquests of Metal Man, excited for us all to be going to Tramore, a place most of them had known only in their wildest imagination.

Planning now began in earnest for the venture. The issue of bathing suits was soon raging.

"Can you wear a bathing suit to hop around Metal Man?" Tess wanted to know.

"I'd imagine so," Mother said, matter-of-factly. "I'm sure he wouldn't hold it against you."

"But I don't have a nice one," Tess whined. "Just that ugly auld thing Mrs. Griffith sent us; sure it must have been worn by a nun. Might as well wear a habit. I want a nice two-piece bathing suit with red and pink roses; I want Metal Man to know that I'm not just any auld hopper."

"I don't think that'll be a problem, dear," Mother replied. "Even Metal Man is not that much of an eejit." The rest of the sisterhood exchanged knowing glances, giggling and nudging each other; I was left wondering what I was missing.

In spite of the bathing suit anxiety, hopping quickly became the new obsession of the sisterhood. They practiced hopping around the giant sycamore tree in our mucky farmyard, neglecting their chores and getting in trouble with Mother.

"I don't care what Mammie says," Tess pouted. "I'm gonna ask Hanna Dalton to make me a bathing suit from Mrs. Griffith's summer dress with the red and pink roses. I'll borrow it from my Christmas turkey money. I'll bet Metal Man will notice me then."

Bernie, still pretending to be above it all, hissed, "Oh, bloody hell, Tess! Give over with yer Metal Man talk! Ya know Mother can't afford bathing suits for us. I just want to ride that carnival rollercoaster to death for about two hours. See how fast it can go."

"You go ahead, Bernie, have a blast," Rosie said. "I'm gonna swim in the ocean and ride the waves back to shore; doesn't cost a penny. I hear it's great craic."

"What about you, Noreen?" Mother asked, aware that our middle sister was not likely to elbow her way into the conversation. "Is there some favorite thing you want to do in Tramore?"

"I'd like to collect seashells and make you a necklace for your birthday," Noreen said gently, then turned to me and said, "What do you want, Billy?"

"I want to get my very own bumpin'car," I yelled. "An' I want to smash into every other car at the carnival till we're one big smash-up. Bam! Bam!"

"That sounds awful," Tess whined. "Mammie, I don't think ya should let Billy do that. He might get hurt real badly."

"Yeah, well, it's one heck of a lot better than hopping around Metal Man on one leg," Bernie interjected. "An' he won't be making a show of himself in a skimpy red bathing suit to do it."

This sparked another round of insults and taunts between Bernie and Tess, which Mother had to break up, as usual.

Josephine, our serious oldest sister, already eighteen, was away at convent school in Arklow. She'd miss all the fun, as usual. Her absence left space for another passenger in the van, so Mother invited Angela Dalton, her good friend from nearby Carrig, to join us on the Tramore outing—an indulgence that was already the talk of the community.

Like most of my mother's friends, Angela was single, in her mid-thirties, and carried the traditional "man's work" on the family farm—plowing behind a team of massive Belgians (that she'd trained herself), planting, weeding, harvesting, and all the grinding labor of animal husbandry.

Unlike most of Mother's friends, she was a tall, buxom red-head, with sparkling green eyes and an open, mischievous smile.

"How about a game of hide-n'-go-seek, Billy," she'd ask as soon as she arrived, kicking off her shoes. Or, "How about getting out the gramophone an' we'll dance a hornpipe?"

She loved to dance, given any excuse. I'd crank up the gramophone and play her favorite hornpipes, reels, and waltzes—eager to see her flying around the kitchen. She'd always insist I dance with her, usually carrying me in her strong arms, until I got too big. Secretly, I had a crush on Angela, and always hoped she'd wait till I grew up so I could marry her.

"All the good men are taken," she'd toss off to Mother, when asked why she never married. Like many attractive women around Rathdargan, it was simply assumed that Angela would spend the rest of her life taking care of her ma and younger siblings. This in spite of having had a successful teaching career before quitting to care for her aging parents.

Angela came to our house once a month on Sunday afternoon, riding her vintage one-speed Raleigh over the hilly six miles and bringing with her a small house gift—usually a Gateaux cake, good-natured banter, and a way of raising everyone's spirits—from Mother all the way down the line to me.

"I've invited Angela Dalton to Tramore with us," Mother announced at supper one night. "She's never been, an' I could use some help with this bunch o' characters." She said this without smiling, knowing we were all delighted with her decision.

"D'ya t'ink Angela will hop around Metal Man with us?" Tess wanted to know. "Cuz if so, she's gonna have ta wear a bathing suit, too. I'm not gonna be the only wan out there looking like an eejit."

"I can't speak for Angela," Mother said. "She'll do whatever she pleases. She's a grown woman with a mind of her own, and I'd appreciate your respecting that and not pestering her about any bathing suit. No one said you had to wear a bathing suit, especially that skimpy thing that you can barely make out. Maybe she'll decide to wear her birthday suit so that you'll look like twins."

This drew howls of laughter and taunts from the rest of the sisterhood, and Tess fled the supper table in tears—a typical reaction of the sisterhood as tension built toward the BIG DAY.

August tenth was over a month away when Mother first announced it, and now the long summer days seemed interminable. We all had our chores, of course, but the sisterhood spent most of their energies in borderline mutiny at the drudgery of farm life and the shortage of money for all the things they coveted.

"When are we gonna sell the pigs?" Bernie wanted to know.

"Not until October," Mother replied. "And ya know that already. It's Fair Day in Rathdargan, October fourth—same as ever."

"Yeah, well," Bernie huffed, "I thought we'd make an exception this year. With Tramore an' all; I need some money. What am I supposed to do?"

"I've told ya already," Mother sighed. "We can't be selling half-fattened pigs so that we can go to Tramore. It's all we can do to buy the feed to fatten 'em, but we have no choice. I'd just have bills from Corrigan's if I sold 'em now."

"It's always the same story around here," Bernie yelled in her belligerent way. "We never can afford *anything* like normal people. It's credit here, credit there, and wait, wait, wait. Wait for October! Wait for November! Wait for December! I'm sick o' waitin'. I'm sick o' being in this godforsaken place, an' I'm sick o' yez all!" With that, she slammed the kitchen door and ran off into the farmyard.

Mother just kept cranking the well-worn handle of the milk churn, saying nothing, staring out at the rain.

Coming up to the first week of August, the frustration with chores kept building, and the sisterhood ran relays pestering Mother about the injustice of life in general and their own dire straits in particular.

"Mammie, do I *have* to milk the cow tomorrow?" Tess wanted to know, for the fourth time in as many days.

"Well of course you do," Mother replied, irked by the question. "Why are ya asking? Ya know it needs to be done. She's not gonna milk herself."

"Yeah, well I think it's time someone else did it," Tess whined. "I'm sick o' milkin' that Kerry cow—she's too hard. My hands are too small , and it's ruining my nails. I hate that cow, an' I hate this farm; we might as well be in prison."

"Would you prefer to muck out the barn?" Mother asked, ignoring Tess's histrionics. "Or grind the turnips for the pigs? Or maybe you'd prefer to clean out the chicken coop? Take your pick! But work is work and it has to be done. The sooner you realize that , the better."

The next day, I happened upon Mother in the cowshed; she had her back to me when I came in, and when she turned, it was clear she'd been crying. I asked her what was wrong, and after quickly wiping her eyes she said, "Well, son, I just found out that the Kerry cow has an udder disease and will have to be put down. I don't know what we're going to do for milk, but I'll figure something. Maybe Lawlors will give us milk on credit till we sell the pigs in October. Please don't say anything to the girls!"

I almost finished for her: "I don't want to bother them. They'll have their own problems soon enough."

Meanwhile, the plans for Tramore went full-speed ahead. No mention of the cow or the impending milk shortage. Tess had managed to get her two-piece bathing suit, handmade by Angela's dressmaking sister, Betty, from the beautiful summer dress Mrs. Griffith—Mother's wealthy and generous friend in New York—had sent.

With the wardrobe issues resolved for the moment, money—in glaring short supply—now took center stage.

Saving money was my specialty in the family, and had been since I knew what money was—at about five. Not only was I hyper-aware of Mother's money worries, but, being the youngest, I was the natural beneficiary of a traditional Irish custom that saw neighbors and relatives confer token gifts on the youngest child, a presumed proxy for the rest of the family, which had no expectation of getting gifts from anyone.

The gifts often came in the form of a two shilling piece or half crown (roughly the equivalent of a quarter or fifty cents); my benefactors were usually my aunts and uncles, or a rare visitor from America. Even the neighbors would sometimes give me silver at Christmas, Easter, or other special occasions.

My intention had always been to share my largesse so as to ingratiate myself to the sisterhood, to play the big shot—as I'd seen Yanks and prosperous relatives do when they came to our house.

The problem was, the money tended to disappear before I ever had a chance to share it. I was always baffled at how quickly my money vanished after the coins first showed up in my sticky palms.

"Billy, how about a piggyback up to the road gate?" This from Bernie or Tess, always after I'd hit the jackpot. "Okay," I'd say, delighted to be included in their outing. "Let's go climb Seacon," a picturesque ridge overlooking our farm.

On the way there, we'd somehow manage to fall down, tumble in the grass, and perform wondrous acrobatic stunts. Up on Seacon ridge, we'd roll around with lots of roughhousing, somersaults, and physical contact.

By the time we got home, we'd all be exhausted, and I'd have forgotten about the gifts from my benefactors. Until I was getting ready for bed.

Then would come that awful, nauseating, empty-pocket feeling of having lost all my money. Again.

Noisy searches would follow my anguished howls at the discovery, and an all-hands-on-deck alarm would be issued in a frenzied pursuit of the missing lucre. But, somehow, none of this elaborate effort ever yielded a single piece of silver.

Slowly, oh, so slowly, I began to suspect, then notice, the coincidence between the playful wrestling matches, boosts over fences, bouncy piggybacks—and the presence of my newfound wealth. The rest of the time, I was roundly ignored, or actively shunned, by the sisterhood.

I was about eight when the sickening truth finally hit me: I was being robbed by the sisterhood, my own family. For days I walked around in a kind of daze, as though I'd fallen off my bike head first, or been kicked in the stomach by a horse. I had trouble breathing, or sleeping, and I was in physical pain at the stark reality of the betrayal. And at my own stupidity for being so slow to catch on.

Mother noticed the change in me immediately. "Billy, is anything the matter? You haven't said a word all day."

"I'm awright," I said. "I just have a bit of a stomach ache," which was true. She felt my forehead, gave me some tea and Jacob's Digestive biscuits, and put me to bed early.

It didn't help. I remained silent for about a week, not eating, not smiling, avoiding the sisterhood, and not hanging around Mother for our usual chats.

"Billy, I'm worried about you," she said. "If you're not better by Monday, I'm going to take you into town to see Dr. Devlin. It's not natural for a boy to stop eating."

Devlin scared the living daylights out of me. He was an alcoholic quack who'd dragged me up and down two sets of stairs when Mother last brought me to his office for an ingrown toe-nail. He wanted to see if I was faking it, I suppose. My shoe was half full of blood before he yanked the offending toenail out with a blunt pair of pliers—torture style. I screamed and nearly passed out in his office, then cried all the way home. That was three years earlier; I was five at the time.

"No, Mammie, not Devlin, PLEASE!" I begged. "I'll be fine. I promise I'll eat soon. I just haven't been hungry, that's all."

After the Devlin threat, I faked eating for another week, then got my real appetite back with a vengeance. I ate everything in sight for several days, to Mother's delight and over my sisters' protests.

"Look at this lad," Bernie complained. "He's gonna eat us out of house an' home. I liked it better when ya went on that hunger strike. Did ya think we'd feel sorry for ya, or what?"

I didn't answer her. I had other things on my mind. For dur-ing my week of silence I had come to realize that the robberies had put a permanent dent in the blind, little-brother trust I had in the sisterhood. And now, I felt catapulted toward the oppo-site—an equally blind sense of mistrust in each and every one of them.

Mother, of course, was exempt, and I never told her about the sisterhood robberies. I was afraid she might kill them.

From that day forth, however, I held the sisterhood collec-tively guilty, and never again let any of them into my confidence about even the most mundane things, like where I was going rabbit hunting or picking blackberries.

By the Tramore outing, I was ten, wise to their gambits, and now kept my money hidden in a safe place: behind a loose stone in the cow shed wall. This granite depository had proven as good as Fort Knox over the years, much to the annoyance of the sisterhood, who spared no effort on bribery, sweet talk, threats, and lavish promises, all geared toward cracking the elusive combination.

But I'd learned my lesson, and security held. By T-day, I'd saved five shillings and six pence—a princely sum by our standards, one that I intended to share on my own terms in Tramore when the time came.

A month of Sundays on, the day finally arrived: August tenth, a gorgeous, sunny morning. A soft breeze blew across the valley, churning the wheat fields in rolling cascades of gold as far as the eye could see.

We were all up early, finishing our chores, making sardine sandwiches, bickering and yelling, breathless with anticipation. We were finally, definitely, going to Tramore. It was not a bad joke, or another one of our fantasies, after all.

Fanning that delirious high-spirited feeling further, Angela burst through the gate with her old Raleigh, sending the border collies into a frenzy, before Mother backed them all down.

Angela sported a bright green dress, newly turned out by her younger sisters, and—true to form—she immediately lit up the farm yard with her hilarious banter. "Kitty," she asked Mother in mock seriousness, "Did ya hear that Metal Man was seen on Grafton Street in Dublin getting a new suit for our arrival? Sure we're going to drive that man to distraction, is what we're gonna do. How is the poor fella supposed to cope with six gorgeous women in one day?" Mother laughed in a way that only Angela could evoke, almost collapsing with mirth before she linked arms and dragged Angela into the kitchen for a cup of tea before the launch.

I was posted as lookout for Murphy's green Vauxhall van. The game of suspense was always the same: Watch every van on the Dargle Road from the time it comes in view past Dwyer's cottage, about two miles before the turn. Follow its every move as it navigates the winding road, with its roof flashing intermittently, barely visible above the thick blackthorn hedges.

If it's a green Vauxhall, and it turns at Crosby's Cross, it's Murphy, and he's coming for us—*to take us to Tramore*. I almost passed out with excitement at the thought.

Murphy was due at 9:00, but I started watching about an hour earlier. I wasn't taking any chances. Well before 9:00, everyone was ready to roll—the whole crew already up at the road gate, a short walk from the house, where the van was to pick us up.

By 9:30, a low-grade anxiety began to tamp down the festive mood. The sky clouded over, with a light rain sweeping in from the Atlantic, to the east. The neighbors who'd come to see us off—Jim Nolan, Tom Duff, Padraig McGee—slowly drifted off with assurances like, "Sure, Murphy's a man of his word. Somethin' must o' happened. He'll be here any minute, now."

Long before it hit, we could see the rain shower crossing the sycamore tree line over Rathdargan village, seat of storied Argyle House, from which the famous King of Leinster, Art McMurrough Kavanagh, defeated the Norman King Richard II, in a series of ferocious battles dating back to the fourteenth century.

But with the rain coming hard and our hopes fading fast, no one was thinking of our glorious history. On the contrary, Bernie gave voice to what we were all thinking: *"Where the hell is that gobshite, Jimmy Murphy?"*

"Do not speak that way of Mr. Murphy," Mother said sharply. "He's a decent, responsible man, an' if he's not here it's because something happened that he couldn't help. So I'll thank you to show some manners and keep your nasty thoughts to yerself."

Bernie just tossed her head and looked defiantly at the empty road.

At around 10:30, Mother threw in the towel: "Well, that's it," she said grimly. "He's not coming. I'm sure there's some good reason; maybe the van wouldn't start. Jimmy never let us down before. Let's get into dry clothes and get some work done. Heaven knows, there's no shortage o' that."

Tess, ever the dramatist, fell down by the road-gate wall and howled at the universe. "This was a *stupid* idea to begin with," she wailed. "I can't believe this is happening to us. After all we did to get ready. What am I supposed to do with this new bathing suit? Now I'll never get to wear it. I hate Jimmy Murphy, and I'll never speak to him as long as I live."

Bernie, always cheered up by Tess's misery, started to laugh, almost hysterically. "Give over will ya! Stop that awful racket before ya wake the dead. Do you really think Murphy cares if ya ever speak to him? Fat chance he'd even notice. An if ya could have seen yourself in that ridiculous bathing suit, you'd know he was doin' ya a favor by not showin' up." The others chipped in their nasty rejoinders, until they grew bored with their own meanness.

Angela, always the optimist, hugged Tess and tried to cheer the rest of us up: "Why don't we all go down to the house, make some tea, and I'll bake some of your favorite scones—you know the ones, with raisins, nutmeg, and cinnamon? Then we can all have high tea on a low table; act like we're in Tramore after all. Metal Man will just have to keep that new suit ready for the next time we visit."

No one laughed this time. This was no laughing matter, even with Angela's humor.

Soaking wet, we withdrew to the farmhouse to dry out and face the stark reality. Back at the farmyard, the dogs greeted us like long lost heroes, but soon adopted our somber mood.

The farm buildings looked drab and forbidding, the mourning doves cooing in the sycamores sounding a chorus of despair and desolation.

Back in the house, the turf fire was still alive in the hearth and gave off a familiar, comforting scent as we crowded into the kitchen. We were used to setbacks and delays, so we knew we'd get over this one.

Good as her word, Angela made her special scones over the open hearth, warming up the kitchen and lifting the mood. Mother made tea, and we all ate the delicious scones in silence, breathing easier, even laughing again. The rain stopped, the sun came back out, and our spirits picked up a bit.

One by one, the sisterhood drifted off to various chores around the farmyard. Tess, who had two pet lambs demanding to be fed, sighed and said, "Back to reality," as if it she were going to the gallows.

Rosie had neglected to clean the chicken coop for over a week and was ordered by Mother to, "Do it now!" Noreen slipped off to her garden plot behind the farmhouse without a word. No one complained anymore or made a fuss. The silence—so uncharacteristic—was heavier than any tears or anger they might have expressed.

Finally, at noon, dishes washed and hope abandoned, Angela pulled the Raleigh out of the shed. "Don't worry, Kitty," she said, still smiling. "It was just not meant to be today. Another time; I'm sure of it. God bless." Then she disappeared beyond the iron gate to a brief chorus of half-hearted goodbye yips from the border collies.

After Angela left, Mother changed her clothes and went back to work, her patented response to bad news. Surrounded by my brace of the border collies, I ambled down to my secret hideaway in the wilderness, numb with disappointment. All I could think of was the bumper cars and the soft-serve ice cream, which now might never be.

I wondered if Murphy had forgotten, got the day wrong, or if the Vauxhall wouldn't start. Without anything to do—Mother had forgotten to assign me any chores for a change—I drifted back up to my lookout post, staring in a daze at the Dargyle Road, cursing Murphy and our bad luck.

Two hours into this black rant, I suddenly jerked awake in disbelief as I thought I spotted the green Vauxhall turning at Crosby's Cross.

Delirious with joy, I sprinted for the kitchen, where Mother was baking bread, flour all over her calloused hands. I came tearing through, screaming at full throttle: "Mammie! Mammie! Murphy's van just turned at Crosby's Cross. He's COMING! Get dressed, quick! quick!" I ran around the farmyard, shouting at the top of my lungs, like the angel Gabriel. I was received by the sisterhood in exactly that same spirit.

They whooped for joy, dashed about, and scrambled like flushed pheasants to get ready all over again and race for the road gate, hope restored. Though by now it was 2:00 p.m., there was never a question of calling the whole thing off. If Mother had even tried, she'd surely have had a full-scale mutiny on her hands.

Murphy pulled up and stepped slowly out of the van, a downcast look in his dark blue eyes. He was a tall man, well over six feet, with broad shoulders filling out his tweed jacket, and brown curls peeking out from under a leather cap.

He owned a fifty-acre farm a few miles outside the village; the taxi was a side business to raise some cash during the summer months. He was the oldest of five, the only male, and had borrowed against the farm to educate his four younger sisters and make sure they had all escaped the drudgery of marrying a farmer. His ma had died suddenly—heart attack—a few years earlier, leaving him the sole caregiver for his da, an abusive, life-long drunk who'd been diagnosed with dementia, which had lately manifested itself in vicious rants and a dangerous habit of night-walking on the busy N7 motorway.

"I'm so sorry, Mrs. Hogan," Murphy blurted out, looking suddenly gaunt and exhausted. "Bridie Flemming, Da's nurse, had a bit o' an emergency this mornin'—young lad sick—so she never came ta take care o' Da. When I went over ta see what was keepin' her, Da ran off an' tried to drown himself in the Barrow. Nora Flood—my neighbor down the road—found 'im wadin' in and talked him out of it. Saved his life, I suppose. Sure I couldn't just leave 'em dere, n' I couldn't bring 'em wid me, either."

"What did you do?" Mother said, putting a concerned hand on Jimmy's shoulder.

"Well, I have Nora to thank," Jimmy said. "Bless her heart, she came to me rescue again. She came home with us and volunteered to take care o' Da till I got back from Tramore. She absolutely insisted that I come take yous ta da beach, seen as how I'd already let ya down. I feel terrible, knowing how much ya were countin' on the day out."

"Oh, sure yer a great man for coming atall," Mother said. "It would have been completely justified if you'd just didn't show under the circumstances." We all just looked at each other, thinking she couldn't be serious.

"Anyway, here we are," Murphy said, suddenly smiling. "Let's make the most of what time we have left. And I'm not gonna charge ya one penny for this trip. It's on me, for all da trouble I've caused ya."

"No! no!" Mother protested. "I won't hear of it. I insist on paying the full fare. It's only right. It costs you just as much one way or the other." If looks could have killed, Mother would have been an instant casualty as my sisters glared at her in utter disgust.

"Now listen," Murphy said, as we all shuffled impatiently. "Here's what we'll do. I'll just charge for the petrol, not a penny more—about half the regular fare. Dat settles it."

"All right!" Mother smiled. "That's more than generous. But I still think you're shortchangin' yerself. Thank you, Jimmy. Let's go, then. Oh, and by the way, let's go by Carrig and collect Angela Dalton. I know she wouldn't want ta miss this."

When we arrived at Dalton's farm, I was assigned the job of running up the long, rocky laneway to the farmhouse to fetch Angela. Out of breath and feeling foolish and shy, I was confronted by a pack of terriers and borders at the farmyard gate. Old Mrs. Dalton, stooped and frail, peered at me over the half-door , straining to understand who I was and what I wanted.

After blurting out some incoherent explanation, she directed me to a distant meadow, where Angela was back at work. I saw her in the distance long before she saw me, her red hair bobbing in a ponytail under a blue bandana, raking hay with her majestic Belgian mares. Striding along in her blue overalls, I thought she was the picture of beauty—the kind you saw on newsreels and posters—fluid and energetic, a natural part of the summer landscape.

When she spotted me, she turned and said, "Billy, I knew ya couldn't leave me for long. See. Love conquers all." Then she set down the reins, ran over and swept me up, swinging me around in a circle, which I found exciting and embarrassing, as I blurted out the account of Murphy's delay.

She didn't hesitate for a moment, though it was an ordeal for her to break off, unyoke the horses, water them, and put them out to pasture before washing up and changing, one more time.

The reversal took almost an hour. The van idled at the end of the lane, its passengers waiting impatiently. I killed time in the farmyard, tossing sticks for the border collies to retrieve.

Angela emerged from the thatched farmhouse looking her splendid self. Back in her high heels and stylish green dress, her legs looked longer than ever, her red hair reflecting the afternoon sun. Walking down the long, rutted lane, Angela took my hand, her perfume wafting over me, and I imagined just the two of us off to Tramore, with me impressing her with my daredevil stunts as a bumper car ace.

"I knew Metal Man would not give up on us today," she announced triumphantly to the gang. "He'll be all the more eager to see us after havin' to wait a bit. Men are like that, ya know." We all laughed uproariously, now back in the groove, receptive to Angela's sassy entry lines.

The back of the van was full with our family, so—much to my disappointment—Angela sat up front with Murphy, wanting to know all about the events of his morning—his poor, suffering da, Nora Flood, and the trials of caring for a mental patient. I sat by myself in the back, feeling miserable, my girl ignoring me for another man—someone she'd just met.

It was only eighteen miles from Carrig to Tramore, as the crow flies. Driving through the endless array of small market towns was no crow flight, however. Thick herds of cows and sheep clogged each two-mile stretch in the late afternoon, and summer vacationers strolled leisurely across the narrow streets, sticking their heads in the window for a chat with Murphy, who seemed to be popular with everyone, not just Angela.

For his part, Murphy seemed to know everyone's name and have a special word for one and all. "Tell (Paddy, Sheila, Tom, Darby, etc.) I sent me best. Tell 'em they should stop in for a cup o' tay next time they're out our way."

We finally escaped the snail's pace of Waterford City and headed out the coast road for Tramore Bay. It started to rain again, just a mist at first, then picking up to a steady, darkening downpour. We'd had sun and rain all day, so we were not too discouraged, but it was not how we'd imagined our arrival in Paradise.

Mother announced that it was exactly 4:30 when, at last, we pulled up to the famous beach.

The first thing I spotted was the giant merry-go-round, right across the road from the Strand. And sure enough, there they were: three piers off on the distant headlands, with the giant Metal Man—tall as Sugarloaf Mountain, it seemed—pointing out to sea through the swirling mist.

Up and down the beach, tiny huts served as change rooms for vacationers and, in spite of the rain, the sisterhood and Angela made a beeline for them. They hadn't come this far to miss their chance to impress Metal Man with those skimpy bathing suits and, if he liked what he saw, perhaps be delivered that elusive prince at rainbow's end.

As it happened, the pier and its celebrated sentry were located on the most distant headland, almost a mile from the beach where we'd changed. No one seemed to know any direct pathway, so we bushwhacked our way there through a tangle of furze, thistles, and brambles, arriving disheveled, scratched, and bruised.

That turned out to be the least of our troubles. For it so happened that the entire perimeter of the pier—presumably the "hopping zone"—was cordoned off with barbed wire fencing and official looking signs reading, "PRIVATE PROPERTY. NO TRESPASSING!"

A herd of Black Angus cows grazed in the field by the fencing, and a fierce-looking roan bull with a white face and a ring in his nose started toward us, bent on protecting his harem. He pawed the ground, made terrifying snorting sounds, and charged the fence—banging against it several times with his two sharp horn stumps.

Tess and Rosie screamed; Bernie, trying to be tough, laughed in her nervous screech, and Mother slapped her sharply across the face: "Stop that, you silly girl! Don't ya think things are bad enough without you screeching like a banshee?" Bernie went silent, putting on her "you-can't-hurt-me" face. Angela hugged her and said, "It'll be all right, a Cushla. We're still gonna have lots o' fun. Ta hell with Metal Man."

We stood around in disbelief for a few minutes before the pitiful truth sank in: There would be no hopping around Metal Man today, or any other day. Whoever had put up that barbed wire fence and sign made sure of that.

We trudged back through the thorny furze, the rain coming down in sheets, the wind knifing in from the Atlantic, blowing us off balance like a party of lost drunks. I was running ahead, flying about like a kite; looking back, I could not have imagined a more forlorn-looking procession.

Walking in single file, Tess led in her red- and pink-rose bathing suit; Angela stumbled along at the end, anchoring the pathetic parade, a brave expression of gaiety on her ruddy face, all hopes of finding Prince Charming dashed, perhaps forever. The others, in between, shuffled along in line, wet and miserable, no doubt wondering how all those weeks of dreaming and scheming could turn so abruptly to an utter disaster.

I didn't care a whit about Metal Man. I was delighted that the pier had been closed. It meant I would get to the bumper cars that much faster.

Back at the Strand, the rain had driven everyone else for shelter, but we were beyond caring about comfort. Though no one in our party could swim, we waded into the surf anyway, determined to rescue something from the wreckage—perhaps even have some fun.

The girls shivered, holding on to each other, looking out at the frightening ocean surging toward us. The tide was coming in fast, whitecaps rising ominously, six-foot waves racing each other, then collapsing on the Strand.

Bernie, always a daredevil, waded out to where we could barely see her, then rode the waves in with whoops of joy, giving us all new heart. The rest of us followed her lead and soon we were riding those waves as if we'd been born to the sea. Angela joined in the fun, but Mother just stood on the beach, water nibbling at her ankles, looking worried and hunched against the rain.

I rode a couple of waves, scraped my knees on the sand, thought better of crying, and instead nagged Mother at my whiny best about riding the bumper cars until she snapped, "Well, you'll just have to wait until we're all good and ready; now will ya stop nagging me!"

Her tone was like another slap in the face; she usually treated me with affection and respect, so I assumed I'd done something to upset her. Feeling foolish and alone, I stood in the downpour feeling sorry for myself, harboring mean thoughts. I wished they'd all drown or get swallowed by a whale so I could go on the bumper cars sooner.

Mercifully, the rain abated, one more time. For what seemed like hours, I sat on the wet sand and sulked, watching the sisterhood and Angela cavorting up and down the Strand. Finally, we changed out of our bathing suits, dried off, and headed for the carnival grounds across the street. It was now well past seven o'clock, the sun slowly dipping toward the western horizon.

At the fish-and-chip stand, the delicious odor of the deep fry wafting over us, we suddenly couldn't wait to eat. I still had a half crown left, but I was saving it for the bumper car rides and the soft serve ice cream. I had given no thought to spending my money on food; after all, that was Mother's job. And she'd promised us fish-and-chips: That was a major part of the deal.

We all ordered the delicacy, along with bottles of Corcoran's Orange Soda, and sitting on the rain-soaked benches inside the carnival entrance, we fell upon our meal like a flock of starving crows. The orange fizz tickled my nose and made me sneeze, but I loved the taste and savored every gulp.

I noticed Mother didn't buy anything for herself; maybe she didn't like fish and chips, I thought. She still looked anxious and irritable, not at all like her even-tempered, confident self.

The girls scarfed down the food and bolted for the various rides and stalls. Mother insisted I stay close to her, so I dragged her over to the bumper cars, where I could ride my very own "metal man." I retrieved my half crown from its hiding place in my shoe, paid six pence for the ride, and away I went.

I found several young lads about my age, all bent on the same path of destruction, crashing into anything and everything in our path. We slammed, bashed, spun, crashed again, went for broke on the last car to bump us, and started the cycle all over again. I signed up for three more turns and was going for a fourth when Mother called a halt to my glassy-eyed pursuit. She had to drag me away before I came to my senses and realized I only had a shilling left.

That's when I saw the raffle booth, advertising a "Ten Pound Grand Prize"—a fortune to my mind. I'd only seen a ten pound note once, at a market fair when someone was paying for a horse. There were several smaller prizes, but all I could think of was that ten pound note. And all I had to do was buy a ticket for three pence.

I bought four tickets while Mother wasn't looking, spending my last shilling, but confident that I would walk away with the Grand Prize and a chance to treat everyone to all sorts of goodies and all the rides they wanted. I was bound and determined to be a hero to the sisterhood, to show them that I didn't hold their thievery and deception against them, although I definitely did. But it was Angela I really wanted to impress.

When Mother came back, I told her I'd bought a ticket. She sighed, shook her head in disbelief at my spendthrift ways, and sat to wait for the raffle.

I had my four red tickets with black trim—numbers 190 through 193. A lanky, scruffy-haired man with a hook nose and a scar on his left cheek—tattoos of naked ladies and snakes wrapped around his forearms—rolled the drum and asked a small boy up front to pluck out a ticket. The boy did as he was told, then called out the winning number.

It was not one of mine; it was one of the smaller prizes, so I didn't pay much attention. A gray-haired lady near the back claimed the prize, with screams of joy and the applause of her noisy friends. About six more winners followed, all with small prizes and great fanfare.

Finally, the draw for the Grand Prize was up, and I was all ears. Tattoo ran the drum, the boy pulled the ticket, and he called, "*NUMBER 190!*" I checked my tickets in disbelief. I couldn't breathe. I stood up and croaked, "Dat's mine! Dat's my number. 190!" I stumbled toward the front of the line, holding up the ticket shyly, self-conscious and sweating.

Tattoo approached me and rudely whipped the ticket from my hand. He tore a chunk off the zero and pulled me aside, whispering out of the side of his mouth: "This 'ere is a damaged ticket, mate; let me give you a good one instead. In fact, I'll do ya a favor, since ya seem like a nice wee chap; I'll give ya a whole new set o' four. Here ya go. Now, off ya go to the back of the line. I have a raffle ta run 'ere."

Embarrassed and confused, I started to protest, "But, Sir, it's the winning ticket. Number 190. I had the winner!" Tattoo just laughed and turned away, muttering, "Bloody wild imagination on 'im, is wot it is."

The rest of the townies hanging around the booth joined him in the jeering and hooting. What could be funnier—a culchie being hustled by a wily carney? I stood there staring at Tattoo, fighting back the tears, feeling desperate, having no idea of what to do next. Should I throw a screaming fit? Sometimes this worked with Mother. I also thought of throwing rocks, if I could find any. That sometimes evened things up when the sisterhood did something beyond the pale.

My desperate reflections were suddenly interrupted when someone in the back shouted, "Wait a feckin' minute! Not so fast dere, Mister! I saw dat. Dat's my friend, Billy Hogan, an' he had da winnin' ticket. Pay him 'is money!"

It was Murphy, standing alone by the side of the tent, his piercing blue eyes flashing in anger as he moved forward to confront Tattoo. At first taken by surprise, Tattoo quickly recovered his swagger and took a threatening step toward Murphy. "Whadyamean?" he asked in his high-pitched voice. "Are ya suggestin' I cheated?"

"I not suggestin' ya cheated," Murphy said, standing his ground. "I'm sayin' it straight out: Ya cheated this young lad here. It's plain as day. He had da winnin' ticket, da wan ya tore up, an' I saw ya do it wid me own two eyes. So why don't ya just pay 'im da ten quid an' be a good bloke?"

"Right!" Tattoo smirked, stepping closer to Murphy till his hook nose was just inches above the peak of the leather cap. "An' if I don't, wot ya gonna do 'bout it?"

"Listen," Murphy said, never taking his eyes off Tattoo. "There's two ways we can do this: da easy way or da hard way. I t'ink ya know what I mean."

"I don't know wot yer talkin' about," Tattoo smirked. "Easy or 'ard, all the same to me. I have a raffle to run, now if ya'll excuse me."

As he moved to get by, Murphy stepped in front of him, blocking his path. They were practically nose to nose when Murphy said, "Here's the easy way. Pay this lad the ten quid, and we'll walk away happy. The hard way? Ya don't want to know about, but let me give ya a hint—you'll end wishin' you'd have paid 'im da money. Do ya follow me?"

"I think yer threatening me with extortion," Tattoo said, "That's wot I think. An' if ya don't scram right now, I'll 'ave to throw ya out with me bare hands. D'ya follow...?"

Before Tattoo could say another word, he found his feet come off the ground as Murphy picked him up by the lapels and slammed him against the tent pole, as if he were a sack of feathers.

Murphy glared at Tattoo and said, in a deadly low register, "This is the beginning of what hard looks like. And ya sure don't want to see the end. Now for the last time, I'm telling ya, pay up!"

By now a crowd had gathered, and several people started chanting: "Kill 'im! Kill 'im! Kill 'em!"

Murphy released Tattoo from his farmer's grip and held up his hands, calling for calm. "No need for that," he said. "Mister" (he leaned over and asked Tattoo his name) "Palfer here has made a mistake and wants to make amends. Isn't that so, Mister Palfer?"

The crowd had now surrounded Tattoo in a tight circle. Several hard-looking youth had stepped up to the front, eager to mete out some rough justice—not caring much for the niceties of due process.

Tattoo's dark eyes flitted about, like those of a cornered animal looking for an escape route. Finding none, and seeing the reality of his situation, he lowered his arms, spread his hands in a resigned gesture, and said, "All right, fellas, an honest mistake may hav' been made 'ere. It's 'ard to keep everythin' straight round 'ere with everyone yellin' an' screamin'. I'd hate ta disappoint yer wee friend 'ere, so tell ya wot. I'll give 'im a fiver, an' we'll call 'er quits. Whadyasay?" With that, he pulled out a crumpled fiver, smiled at me , and stuck out his hand to shake.

I couldn't believe it. Tattoo, the shifty thief, was actually going to pay me a fiver? I reached for it eagerly, delighted, and Tattoo pulled me around the flap of the tent, his arm around my shoulder in an affectionate gesture. And that's when he made his move.

He grabbed me by the hair, yanked my head back and hissed, "One more word about a tenner, an ya'll never see yer Mammie again. I know where ya live, and I'll come when ya least expect. Got it! Now scram!"

I lurched out of the tent, sobbing in confusion and rage. I ran to Murphy and he put his powerful arms around me as I poured out Tattoo's vile threat:

"He says he's gonna kill Mammie if I don't take the fiver. Gonna come ta our house when we don't expect 'im."

Murphy didn't say a word, released me quickly and walked over to where Tattoo stood, smiling benevolently. In one fluid motion—so quick that I don't think Tattoo ever saw it coming—Murphy jammed two fingers into the carney's throat—which instantly disabled him, as if he'd been hit by a stun gun.

The crowd gasped in amazement as Murphy dropped Tattoo's limp body in front of the tent, where he lay for a several minutes as the crowed milled about, speculating on his chances of survival.

Then he opened his eyes and sat up, looking about with a dazed expression.

"Wot happened?" he asked. "Where am I?"

Murphy knelt to check out Tattoo's eyes at close range, the curious onlookers pressing in. "Move back!" Murphy commanded, now in full charge. "Give him some air." He cupped Tattoo's scarred face in his left hand hands, then slapped him vigorously, open palm and backhand—much to the amusement of the crowd—and asked: "What's yer name?"

"Rudy Palfer," Tattoo said, still looking woozy.

"Where are you?" Murphy asked.

"In Tramore. At the carnival." Tattoo smiled as he said this, brightening at his prospects.

"Where is the other five quid ya robbed from young Billy Hogan?" Murphy asked, standing over Tattoo.

He staggered to his feet in the face of Murphy's question, realizing this had not been just a bad dream.

He stared at Murphy, then at me, and back to Murphy, who stood there, waiting.

"I don't remember anything about owing anyone five quid," Tattoo said, acting confused. "An' who's Billy Hogan, anyway?"

Just as it seemed as if Murphy was going for Tattoo's throat again, two muscular young garda arrived on the scene—someone had alerted them—their shiny caps and polished buttons reflecting the sunlight, giving them an impressive, sparkling glow. They inquired about "the disturbance."

Murphy stepped forward and explained: "It's just a misunderstanding, officer. Mr. Palfer here is just about to pay my young friend the five quid he owes 'im. No harm done?" He winked broadly at Tattoo, who nodded his shaggy head in sullen capitulation.

"Yer man 'ere is right, Sir," Tattoo scowled. "That's about the size of it. His friend 'ere is a lucky wee lad—won the Grand Prize, ten quid, it woz. That's a lot o' scratch for a young un."

With that, he handed me the second pink five pound note, with the large, bald man on its front, dressed in an elaborate green robe holding a staff in his right hand. It was my second fiver in less than an hour. I stared at the two bald heads for a long time, trying to absorb what had just transpired.

There have been other rare moments of triumph when the gods of fortune have smiled, and that elusive, longed-for thing has tilted my way. But none have ever felt better than that August moment at Tramore when Tattoo found religion and handed over the final part of my Grand Prize.

Mother had seen it all from her seat in the back. Now she came forward, thanked Murphy profusely for what he'd done, then turned to me with an emotion I couldn't make out—a cross between worry and restrained laughter.

She just said, "Now that yer rich, ye'll have ta find a real deposit box for that tenner. And I know I don't have to tell ya to be careful how ya spend it." I laughed with relief, realizing she'd known about my hiding place all along, probably the robberies, too, and that she'd never punished the sisterhood, trusting me to handle it on my own.

We rounded up the girls, and I didn't say a word about the raffle, at first. They were all broke by now, still bitter about Metal Man, the bull, Murphy's delay, the rain, and now, a premature end to the outing. At times like these, they had a habit of turning mean, becoming a nasty mob, blaming Mother, me, then the universe—usually in that order—for their misery. They now turned it on with a vengeance, demanding more money: for rides, games, raffles, and ice cream.

Mother played it straight, telling them the truth—that she, too, was broke and that we'd just have to go home. No money for supper. She would barely have enough to pay Murphy for the petrol, even with the generous discount.

Seeing they were on the verge of going completely feral, I made my move—hands in the air, as I'd seen Mother do, clearing my throat before saying: "Hush up! Please! I have somethin' I want ta tell yez!"

Tess glared at me and yelled, "Why would anywan care what ya have ta say? Little brat! We're broke n' hungry, and now we have ta go back to dat prison called home. So stuff a sock in it. I don't wanna hear it."

Bernie, delighted at the chance to rip into Tess, stepped up and said, "You stuff a sock in it, Tess. Maybe two, with your big mouth. Billy is tryin' ta speak. So just shut up, the lot a yez!"

"I won the Grand Prize at da raffle," I crowed. "TEN POUNDS, an I wanna take yez all for yer favorite treats. Whatever ya want ta eat, I'll pay for EVERYTHIN'." I held up the two fivers for all to see, making sure to keep them out of reach of their grasping fingers. After an initial moment of awe and disbelief, the shrieks of delight could be heard two blocks away.

Mother told them the story then, in fragments. It would be pieced together later, embellished over the years, and eventually mythologized almost to the level of Metal Man. After all, we'd just won our own pot of gold. An essential part of the myth would always include Murphy, of course, and how he'd learned martial arts—Kyusho-Jujitsu—from a visiting Japanese master who had taught him the manly art of "pressure point fighting."

Now I was able to live out my grandest fantasy: play the big shot and invite the entire sisterhood and Mother out on the town, and not just any town. This was *Tramore, the place we'd long-since dreamed about.*

Counting heads, we discovered Angela had turned her ankle stepping off the rollercoaster in her high heels. Bernie said she was down at the beach, soaking her injured limb in the salt water.

That's where we found her, sitting on a rock, nursing a pain-ful-looking sprained ankle. We told her the good news—all talking over each other—about Murphy's heroics and my offer to treat everyone.

She jumped up, winced, tears running down her cheeks, then laughed off the pain and said, "Well, ya see, Metal Man must have noticed us, after all. Probably felt sorry for us and set Billy up with the Grand Prize. Let's all go to the Strand Hotel and have high tea! I've wanted to do that as long as I can remember."

I smiled at Angela and said, "Well, I'm payin' for everywan today. Dat's somethin' even Metal Man can't do. Ya have to be a rich toff, like me."

She hugged me and said, "I knew I'd find a rich man if I just waited long enough." She leaned on me until we got to the boardwalk, then limped along by herself, a high heel shoe in each hand.

We spotted Murphy leaning against the bonnet of the Vauxhall, which he'd parked in front of the elegant Strand Hotel. He was smoking a Sweet Afton, looking like an ad for the brand, taking in the sunset.

When he saw the entourage coming up the boardwalk, with Angela limping, he tossed the cigarette and ran toward us, offering to help. She waved him off with a smile and said, "Don't worry. If I need ta lean on ya, I will. It's always nice to have a good, strong man around. And Metal Man didn't seem up to it today."

Murphy joined us for high tea after a lot of coaxing from Mother: "The least we can do, given what you did for us and for Billy back there. I don't know how we can ever thank you enough."

"No bother, Ma'am." Murphy said quietly. "The young lad won it fair and square." He took off his cap as he entered the hotel, revealing an unruly head of curls springing forth.

The maître d'hôtel ushered us up to a huge balcony overlooking the ocean. Soon the waiters came, in tuxedos, to take our order. We all said the same thing, almost in unison: "High Tea, please!" The sisterhood got the giggles and had to be disciplined sternly by Mother before they regained control.

They served us on small, ornate tables, one for each of us, with a mouth-watering array of finger sandwiches and confectionery—barmbrack, my favorite from that day forth—currant scones with whipped cream, sticky buns, ginger bread, and jelly rolls. Angela and Mother each had a glass of sherry, which they sipped slowly, after clinking glasses and winking at each other. Murphy waved off an offer to join them in a drink of his choice. "Still have ta get us home safe, ya know," was all he said.

The Strand tea went well beyond even our most fevered fantasy. We bolted down every last morsel, clearing our plates in minutes. The waiters promptly refilled the trays, which we also devoured—at which point Mother called a halt, looking around, embarrassed.

The bill was presented on a leather tray decorated with a big, red rose. I made a display of calling for the tray, "That's mine," looking at the bill, and trying not to pass out. It was for FIVE POUNDS!—ten shillings each, ten more for the sherry, plus a ten percent "gratuity," which Mother explained to me as a way of "thanking the waiters for their service." "Ten shillings is a lot of thanks," I said. "How come we have ta give 'em money? Don't they get wages for working here?"

"I'll explain it to ya *later*," she said; her code word for, "When you're old enough to get it…"

The bill was half my entire Grand Prize. It was the same as the price of a yearling calf, two lambs, or a brood sow. I couldn't believe we'd just blown that on a *tea*.

No one said a word as I looked the bill over, feeling very grown up—like some blend of older brother and Da rolled into one—and stricken.

I tried to look confident, like I was used to throwing money around like this. I reluctantly handed over half my pot of gold to the waiter—one of the fivers. No change. I was terrified when he came marching back, smiling, with the leather tray. Did he need more money? Perhaps the other fiver? I slumped in relief when I saw it was just the embossed "Strand Hotel" receipt for the five pounds. It was decorated in a shamrock of mints, which I passed around—my final grand gesture as host.

I still felt rich, but somehow I felt cheated, too. Half my wealth had just gone, whoosh! Like that! It would take years for me to even begin to reconcile the paradox of feeling so utterly wretched at what should have been my moment of greatest triumph.

With the tea under our belts, it was time to head for home. Murphy had been sitting beside Angela during the meal, and now he helped her stand, and she leaned on his arm all the way to the car. He tucked her into the passenger's seat beside him, and wrapped her in a beach towel, making much of soothing her injured ankle.

On the long ride home, the sisterhood was in great form, competing for my attention, when all I wanted was Angela's. She was sitting directly in front of me, close to Murphy, her red hair almost touching his auburn curls.

At a red light in Waterford City, during a lull in competing plans for outings to Seacon with me, Murphy turned to Angela and said: "How about we go dancing in Kilkenny as soon as the ankle heals up? Ya know what they say: 'Tis an ill wind that blows nobody any good.'"

We leaned forward for an Angela quip that never came. Instead, she paused, looked directly at Murphy and said, "Ya know somethin,' Jimmy? In my experience, *they* are usually right. Kilkenny it is, a week from Sunday; I should be all set by then. I hear The Johnson Show Band is playing at The Point." They sat there, staring straight ahead, before someone behind us blasted the horn, startling Murphy into the realization that he was blocking a busy intersection.

We sat silently in the back, the sisterhood nudging each other, exchanging winks and meaningful glances. I had no idea what was going on. I was thinking about ill wind and what he meant by "blows nobody any good."

Our first stop was Carrig, Angela's family farm. The narrow, rutted laneway was impassable to motor cars, so Murphy offered to carry Angela up to the farmhouse.

"A million thanks, Kitty! Girls! I'll see yez next Sunday," Angela said, waving to us happily from her perch in Murphy's arms. "Come hail or shine, I'll be there. Billy, be sure ta have da gramophone needles sharpened." Then she blew me a kiss.

For all my good fortune in Tramore that day, my last image of Angela was one that made me miserable until I saw her again: her tanned arms around Jimmy's neck, high heels dangling from her fingers, red hair and green dress billowing in the late summer wind.

ALL SOULS' DAY

ALL SOULS' DAY

ON THE NIGHT IN QUESTION—NOVEMBER 2, 1948—Danny Breen was only five and saw it as the start of a game, a deadly game that sometimes left him in convulsions of terror when the sisterhood got carried away.

"Hush up! Did ya hear that?" Bridie, the oldest and chief terrorist, always heard it first, that bloodcurdling wail that put the fear of God into all six of them. "No, what?" his other four sisters would ask as a chorus, knowing full well what was coming. "The scream down in the valley. Oh, sweet Jesus, it must be her," Bridie would affirm, and the rest would join in with creative riffs: "Right. I can hear her now. She's coming this way. I think she's comin' for Danny."

That was the game, of course, with Danny the target; he was the youngest and only male in a family of six, headed by a single mother ("Mammy," who, that night, was away tending to her dying mother—the children's beloved Granny).

Their farm was tucked in the rural outback of Ireland's Leinster province, and the long, dark winter was a juicy opportunity for mischief makers. As anyone growing up in the country knows, nocturnal animal cries can be any feral creature out there in the dark: a vixen calling to her kits, a goat in rutting season lusting for a mate, a rabbit caught in a trap. But given the sisters' well-honed theatrics, these sounds were invariably converted to one of two nightmarish apparitions: Satan or the banshee.

Satan, the devil, known to all Catholic children as evil incarnate, was always thirsty for the blood of young boys like Danny. Armed with horns, a long, forked tail, and wolf-like fangs, he had a nasty habit of ripping his victims asunder, one limb at a time. The sisterhood used him sparingly, reserving him for special occasions, like saving the joker for a trump moment in a card game.

This night, though, featured the banshee, who was, for Danny, a lot scarier than the devil. She was rumored to be a Celtic goddess, a ghostly harbinger of ill tidings, usually a death in the family. To Danny, the banshee was a real woman, but unspeakably weird.

Danny's aunts and uncles swore they'd seen her on many occasions, and he had no reason to doubt them. They'd described her as young and beautiful. Wronged in some horrid fashion— by a lover, no doubt—her tormented spirit roamed the earth, combing her golden locks and keening.

In those awful moments, when the death of some loved one was nigh, she'd glide past your door, appear in your mirror, stand by your bedside, and then fade away. And God help you if you heard her wailing, as they all just had.

The stage for this night's drama was set months earlier, when Granny started having small strokes that ended in profuse nosebleeds and temporary, but total, memory loss—memories that would then have to be slowly restored, one painful conversation at a time.

Granny's farmhouse was visible across the valley from the Breen's house—directly in the foothills of majestic Mt.

Leinster—where Danny's mother had grown up, before she married Pete Breen and moved to Killgoran, three miles away.

Granny had left Cahill Farm to Aunt Brigid, Mammy's younger sister, who lived there now, cultivating the small farm with her husband and seven children. This became the arrangement after both sisters, immigrants to Chicago in the Roaring Twenties, returned to Ireland during the Great Depression to raise their families.

Jo, as everyone called her, formerly Josephine Cavanagh, was raising Danny and his sisters on a rocky, hard-scrabble farm without the presence of their da, who had been killed on a building site in Gravesend. Still, as the oldest daughter and consummate caregiver, every time Granny fell ill, Mammy would rush to the rescue, driving her pony and trap up the dark, steep roads—convinced she was the only one capable of saving the day. Mammy was like this about most things, so Aunt Brigid and her easygoing husband, Jim, just went along.

The communication between the two farms was simple, but effective: When Granny fell ill, Aunt Brigid would hang out a white sheet on her clothesline, which all could plainly see from Killgoran—if it was daytime. If it happened at night, she'd blink the kerosene lantern three times—the SOS signal. All hands on deck, pony harnessed, Mammy barking instructions, sister Bridie in charge, and be quick about it.

The children were used to the drill, but in his heart of hearts, Danny dreaded these rescue missions. They'd happened several times in the course of a year, all false alarms. Granny would be right as rain in a few weeks, joining the family for Sunday dinner after mass, all decked out in her fashionable hats and heirloom brooches.

She smelled of exotic perfume, brought sweets for all, and read Danny stories that were enchanting and memorable. Afterward, the whole family would drive her back to Cahill Farm in the pony and trap, the entire crew squeezed in like sardines for the outing. By then, it would be usually be dark, and Danny—ever since he was a baby—would invariably fall asleep and have to be carried up to bed after they got home. He loved those Sunday visits, loved Granny—in his five-year-old way—and prayed to St. Anthony for her recovery each time she fell ill.

He never even thought about her dying, even when she was felled by the strokes with increasing frequency. That's why that Saturday afternoon didn't seem any big deal when Mammy rushed, once more, for Cahill Farm. For him, it had been just one more futile rescue mission, one more night to dread being at the mercy of the sisterhood.

As it turned out, it was a night unlike any other—and someone or *something* was determined to make it so. And this night, it was not the banshee, after all: It was something else, something that even the sisterhood could not have conjured up.

November second happens to be All Souls' Day— known in Ireland as the Day of the Dead—the day Roman Catholics celebrate the departed and pray for the sanctification of their souls. This was on the safe assumption that they wouldn't die in a perfect state of grace: more likely they'd die as works in progress, mere mortals who'd require a probationary stint in Purgatory.

In the meantime, it might soothe their tribulations if the living were to set a place at the table, leave some food out, and pray for their acceptance at the pearly gates. That was the children's understanding of why November 2 was a special day.

And night.

In addition to Granny's imminent death and the wailing coming from whatever-it-was down in the valley, consider the setting and the season that November night, a Northwestern Atlantic island in the dead of winter: dark, darker, darkest—that's what the Irish winter ushered in. A tangible, inky blackness that is unimaginable to those born with electricity and modern lighting amenities.

Drape that darkness over the souls of the ancestors, on furlough from Purgatory, craving a decent meal and a bit of warmth at the hearth, and you have the perfect setup for aspiring young tricksters, especially when they happen to be five sisters—all under fourteen—with a much younger brother at their behest, home alone.

"Listen, here she comes," Bridie whispered, turning off the lantern and lighting a candle, the better to see the dancing shadows. This was par for the course, so Danny was braced for another medley of horrors, aware that the sisterhood seemed even more animated than usual—giggling, whispering, squealing.

That's when the wailing stopped abruptly, as if passing the baton to the massive border collie, Captain—known to the family as "Cap"—his ferocious, attack-style barking amplified across the ghostly silence of the farmyard. And that's when the game stopped being a game, even for the sisterhood.

Cap was Danny's fearless protector and edgy bodyguard in all matters of physical danger. That's why Danny felt mostly relief when he first heard the familiar bark at the gateway entrance to the farmyard. Cap was a huge, broad-shouldered border collie, always spoiling for a fight, sniffing out any lurking predators. His strategy was simple: attack first, and never let up until his master called him off. Above all, *win the fight*; then beg forgiveness with a wag of your white-tipped tail and a wide "aw, shucks" grin.

Danny loved the big border's swagger and total self-confidence, qualities he couldn't even imagine in himself. He felt perfectly safe in Cap's presence, day or night. In fact, it was the only time he felt safe—given his pitiful role as the ball in the sisterhood's loaded game of five on one.

Cap's barking suddenly changed register, becoming more intense, more of a growl, deep in his huge barrel chest. Even children know that dogs can sense things that humans are not privy to, so they all felt a new presence in the pitch-dark farmyard. For once, everyone—not just Danny—was absolutely petrified.

Bridie had taken up her lookout post at the small, gable-end window—more like a peephole that would accommodate only one body at a time—in the upstairs bedroom. The rest were huddled under the window, clinging to each other in terror on the wooden floor, as the terrible racket in the farmyard intensified.

Mammy had told them to be on the lookout from the window, in case the worst happened. If Granny died, she'd signal with three blinks of the lantern. Now, as they clamored for a peek at the action with Cap, they forgot all about Granny, Mammy, and her mission of mercy.

The moon slid up from behind Mt. Leinster, lighting the farmyard all the way to the red iron gate—about thirty yards away. Maggie, the second oldest sister, was taking her turn at lookout. "Oh, Jesus," she gasped, "There's somethin' comin' through the gate, but I can't see it. Whatever a tis, it's gettin' the best o' Cap. He's backin' down the lane."

At that, the sisters screamed in unified terror, "What are we goin' to do? Jesus, Mary, and Joseph, what are we goin' to do?"

Danny cringed by the wall, hugging his knees, listening to his fierce protector's mortal struggle.

Cap's bark changed again—from a defensive growl to a high-pitched whine—a cringing, defeated whine—the kind they'd heard from his canine challengers dozens of times as they surrendered and fled before his lethal onslaughts.

The gateway that had just been breached was a second iron barrier—designed to keep animals out—at the end of a long laneway leading to the farmhouse.

The Breens was the only homestead on the eastern side of the Mt. Leinster foothills, so their isolation was stark and absolute. No other neighbor within shouting or screaming distance; no one to call for help. But they'd always felt completely safe, as long as their great fighting border was on guard.

Until tonight.

How could this be happening to such a champion pugilist? What kind of creature, or presence, would it take to intimidate a dog like Cap? Perhaps all the dearly departed barging through the gate at once, skeletal, desiccated, hungry—thirsty for Danny's blood, perhaps, as the sisterhood had suggested earlier.

As these and other horrifying images raced through his mind, Danny fought for his turn at the tiny window; he was just in time to see Cap sliding down the driveway, haunches grinding in the mud, snapping and snarling at some unseen ghoul as he was being driven back, back, until he disappeared under the lookout window, which was directly over the hefty kitchen door. Immediately, Cap's hindquarters began slamming against the door, as though he might shatter the staunch oak timbers.

They could hear him, just below the window, whimpering and snarling, in some kind of death throes with his ghostly foe, as he banged against the door repeatedly, with no more ground to give.

With the exception of Bridie, the sisters were still huddled under the window, tight as a tick, yammering hysterically, wailing in unison, outdoing any creature that might appear. But Bridie, always nerveless, didn't budge from the lookout, and Danny decided on a last ditch move to save his dog.

"Please, someone, come downstairs with me so we can let him in!" he pleaded. "He's gonna die down there. Whatever that thing is, it's gonna kill 'im." He could get no takers, of course. The sisters just clung to each other in the flickering candlelight, like a huddle of traumatized primates in the forest. And there was no way Danny was walking down those creaky stairs alone, not knowing what would be out there once he opened the door.

So no one moved; they just cowered under the window, a whimpering chorus, leaving the valiant border to his fate.

Danny had no idea how long Cap's torture lasted, pinned as he was against the door, but it seemed like a lifetime. Then, suddenly, the battlefield went silent, and no one dared move a muscle.

A moment later, the grandfather clock downstairs struck twelve, its somber chimes amplified in the silent farmhouse. It was midnight, the end of All Souls' Day.

As the big clock fell silent, Bridie's anxious voice broke in: "Look, look, it's the light in Cahill Farm. There a tis: the three blinks. Granny's dead! Oh my God, Granny's dead!" The children started up again in howls of grief and terror. Then, as if on cue, they quickly fell silent.

It took Danny a few moments to remember that Cap had gone silent, too. His first thought: "Maybe he's dead, too, like Granny. Maybe the same thing that got Granny..."

The sisters began to disengage from the huddle, and Danny seized the opportunity to grab Siobhan—his youngest sister—by the hand and drag her downstairs. She didn't protest, just let him lead her in silence.

They opened the heavy kitchen door, numb and jumpy in the ghostly moonlight. Cap streaked past them—a black and white meteor—wet and pungent from his demonic ordeal; inside, he cowered away from them, drool frothing from his mouth, and dove under the table, stinking up the whole house.

Cap stayed there until Mammy came home a few hours later. Even then, she had to coax him out with some milk.

For the next several days, the great dog refused to eat or go outside. Only after some hand-feeding and—unusual for Mammy—a steady dose of kindness did he finally venture forth.

By the end of the week, he responded when Danny called him to help fetch the cows, and by the time they got home, he'd regained most of his swagger. And Danny was back to feeling safe in his presence.

———————

This is a famous ghost story back in Killgoran, having been passed along and embellished hundreds of times over the years, now with a life of its own among local *shanachies*—story-tellers. Several claim they witnessed it with their own eyes, ears, and nose—as did, apparently, the fabled border collie, who, of course, experienced something truly ethereal, as only dogs can.

Danny did notice that, mysteriously, the sisterhood never mentioned Satan or the banshee again. For that, he felt eternally grateful to whatever it was.

HARD TRUTHS

HARD TRUTHS

THE TELEGRAM CAME IN THE late afternoon on a rainy Tuesday in late April, 1958.

Jimmy Dunphy had been delivering mail to this remote farmhouse in the Wicklow Mountain Range for over thirty years, but he still felt a tingle of excitement each time that distinctive little green envelope showed up in his bundle. Hogan's of Rathdargan was the last stop on his route, and he always looked forward to a relaxed chat with Kitty Hogan, full-figured woman of the house. Sometimes—if she was in a good mood—she'd invite him in for a cup of tea and a scone to fuel the long, uphill bike ride home to his cottage on the other side of Sugarloaf Mountain.

Telegram presentation was one of Jimmy's specialties, one he'd polished to a performance art. Unlike regular mail, telegrams meant something was up—and Jimmy loved to watch the faces of people in the grip of suspense. Today he was bitterly disappointed to see that only young Myles, not his mother, was there to share the moment. Was he going to have to waste a performance on this fourteen-year-old upstart? This younger generation had no appreciation of true dramatic talent; most had never even heard of O'Casey, Behan, or Bernie (aka "George Bernard") Shaw, born just over the mountain in Carlow. Too busy traipsing to American cowboy pictures and dance halls. Then again, how were they ever going to learn if their elders didn't show them?

Peering through the rain under his shiny postman's cap and black parka, Jimmy grinned and stepped boldly on to the stage—his own Abbey Theatre. First, he held the prized envelope high for inspection—like a trophy ready for presentation. Rolling it over several times in his arthritic hands, puffing vainly on his unlit pipe, he held the telegram aloft one last time before the final moment of exchange.

Myles Hogan didn't hear the postman's whistle right away; he had his hands full in the cowshed, dosing an ailing calf from a plastic bottle. But the brace of border collies sounded the alarm, nearly flattening him in their raucous scramble for the cowshed door. Myles liked Jimmy Dunphy and usually welcomed his theatrics, but not today. There was too much work to do; he was soaking wet and in no mood to humor the old man.

Finally, with great reluctance, Jimmy surrendered the telegram into Myles's impatient hand. Stung by the rude reception, he turned wearily to face the hilly, wet meadow he'd cut though to reach the farmhouse. No tea. No scones. Not even a glimpse of Kitty Hogan's brunette curls.

Turning abruptly to leave, noticing Jimmy's hangdog expression, Myles felt a pang of regret and tossed off a quick apology: "Thanks, Mr. Dunphy. Sorry to be in such hurry. Hungry calves, ya know…"

Jimmy seized the opening like a lifeline.

"Maybe I should wait till yer mammie has a chance to read it. Ya never know…She might want to send word back…"

It was a clumsy attempt at ferreting out what was in the telegram; Myles knew how the gossip mill worked and had no intention of feeding it.

"No, thanks, Mr. Dunphy. Mammie's busy right now, but I'll let her know your offer."

Jimmy was not so easily put off, especially by a young bucko getting too big for his breeches. "Maybe we should let the mammie decide. Ya never know…"

"That's all right, Mr. Dunphy. Thanks anyway." With that, Myles met the old man's eyes with an unsmiling dismissal, turned, and raced down the steps, tripping over the tangle of border collies stacked up below him, before righting himself and sprinting for the kitchen, where his mother was baking bread over the open hearth.

"Mammie, Mammie, it's a telegram!" he yelled as he barged into the dimly lit kitchen, borders charging in tow. Kitty Hogan looked up from a deep reverie. She was cranking the handle of the bellows, which fed a glowing turf fire. Over it, a covered iron skillet rested. She started, as if coming awake, brushed a wayward curl from her forehead, and nervously wiped her hands in her faded, striped blue apron. A shadow of dread crossed her lined, though beautiful, face.

In Kitty's forty-four years, telegrams had meant only one thing: bad news. The last one had been two years before, announcing that her beloved Aunt Mary—a second mother to her—had died in New York. The one before that, in October of '55, had summoned her to Dublin where Maura, her youngest daughter, had been run over at a crosswalk near O'Connell Street Bridge. She'd died two days later at the St. Vincent's Hospital, without regaining consciousness. Maura was a bright, good-natured girl, just eighteen—the last of the five sisters at Temple Hill Nursing School— all on meager scholarships. She'd only been in the city a week.

Meeting his mother's hazel eyes, Myles handed her the telegram with trembling fingers. Kitty hesitated before reaching for it, took a deep breath, and walked to the dresser at the back of the kitchen. Hours seemed to pass before she eventually opened the drawer, pulled out a paring knife, and slit the green envelope in one swift flick. Even the borders sensed the tension and sat on their haunches, as at feeding time, their gazes riveted on Kitty's every move. She stepped toward the light of the front window, took another deep breath, and plucked out the folded, official note, which she read silently to herself, several times; then, finally, aloud:

"Coming home Friday (May 1). 6 p.m. bus to Enniskerry. Jack."

Tears streamed down Kitty's pale cheeks, dripping on her apron. She swatted them away as a smile erased the shadow, spreading from her lips to her streaming eyes, then to her whole body. She let out a scream of pure ecstasy. "Oh, Jesus, Mary, and Joseph! Jack is coming home. Your father is coming home. Oh, my God! Oh, my God! I knew he would come someday. I knew God would answer my prayers…I just knew it…"

She whirled about the concrete floor in a wild dance of joy that Myles had never seen before, almost knocking him over as she swung her arms wide. Inspired by her exuberance, the borders started to bark, joining the circular dance. Suddenly, Kitty pulled up, self-conscious and blushing, almost childlike. She smoothed the faded apron, brushed back the curls from her forehead, and regained her normal, no-nonsense comportment.

"Now listen, Myles, we have a ton of work to do to get ready. We have only two days, mind you. We'll have to paint the road gate, clip the hedges, and cut all those thistles in the cow field. Oh, and Myles, you'll have to go up to Billy Roach and get a haircut. What would your father say if he saw you looking like that? He'd think I was raising a teddy boy…" She rattled on in this vein, extending the list in her assertive fashion, but Myles had already tuned her out and was walking toward the cowshed to finish his feeding chores.

This was the moment he'd dreaded for two years, ever since he'd quit Enniskerry National School in the middle of the fifth grade to help his mother on the farm.

Myles was the only one in the family who seemed to accept the fact that his father was never coming home. He'd heard the story so many times, with so many variations and subplots, that he felt it was just another fairytale. Kitty had tried to make excuses for Jack and present him as a heroic figure, but Myles never bought the fiction, sensing an unspoken truth: that the real hero was the woman who stuck with him and his older sisters instead of farming them out to relatives, or worse: Killane orphanage, the workhouse in Gorey.

Kitty Hogan was a maddening bundle of contradictions Myles could never figure out. She could be gentle and nurturing, treating Myles as an equal, a partner. Ever since he could talk, she had sought his views on all sorts of grown-up matters, large and small: Should she sell the bonhams or fatten them? Should she plant Furlong's Field with oats or lease it to John McDonald? Should she let the girls go to the dance in Bray on Sunday night? And she wasn't just humoring a child; she really listened to what he had to say and encouraged him to tell her the truth, especially when it was hard.

Like two years ago, when he left the turkey run open, and a fox killed the whole flock; it was their only Christmas cash crop. "Mammie, I have a confession to make." He found her in the middle of baking a cake for supper. "Well, this sounds serious. You look like you've seen a ghost." Myles sat down, fought back tears and spilled the story. "It's all my fault. You told me to lock the gate every time I came out, but I didn't. I just forgot it, like an eejit. And that's when the fox must've slipped in. I never saw him. Just heard the racket and ran in there. It was too late. He'd killed them all and was gone. There wasn't even any blood. Just broken necks. Like I said, it's all my fault, and I don't mind if you whip me with the belt. I deserve it...I'd do anything if it'd make 'em come back...anything. "

Instead of a whipping, she gave him her brightest smile, wrapped her arms around him, and said, "You're a good man, Myles Hogan. Any fool can tell the truth when it wraps him in glory. It's the hard truth that separates the men from the boys. Now, let's have some tea and scones before we have to break the news to your sisters that we have to cancel Christmas this year." As she said this, her voice broke, and she turned away to hide the tears.

This was in sharp contrast to the way she treated the girls, whom she dismissed as a bunch of "gillagoolies." His sisters resented this, of course, and took it out on Myles with fiendish creativity. Knowing his fear of the dark, they seldom missed an opportunity for nightly terror games. Once, when he was about seven, they put a small goat in his bedroom, complete with horns; the devil come to claim his prey. As soon as Myles saw the horns, illuminated by a small lantern, the boy went into screaming convulsions to gales of triumphant giggling from under the bed.

The harsh punishments meted out by his mother only made Myles feel guiltier. He tried to make it up to his sisters by currying favor, but to no avail. It was their mother's approval they craved, not his. But, for them, that approval would always be in short supply.

Myles had always been puzzled by the deference people showed his mother. All sorts of people—men and women, prosperous and poor—seemed to speak of her with a kind of reverence, as they might speak of the bishop or prime minister. There was a magical power that seemed to cast a protective shield around him and his sisters as soon as people knew their names. Being Kitty Hogan's son was special in Enniskerry; everyone seemed to understand that, for reasons Myles could only guess at. "Can I give ya a lift? Ain't you Kitty Hogan's boy?" "Sure, it's all right. Ya can have it for five bob. Aren't you one of the Hogans of Rathdargan?" "Yer mother's a great woman. She done a lot for this country. You must be very proud to be her son." Once he asked her what people meant by this, but she brushed it off with, "Oh, son, we all did a lot for our country in the old days. It's not worth talking about. Now, run down to the lower meadow and bring in the cows!"

But he knew there was more to it. He had seen some of it firsthand.

He recalled the fate of the schoolteacher, Brigid Breen, after she had slapped his oldest sister, Nora, for misbehaving in school. For other children, beatings in the National School were expected and accepted. Except the Hogans. Myles remembered the terrible spectacle of Miss Breen falling on her ample knees on the gravel road, pleading for mercy, as Kitty stood leaning against the stone wall, cool as a lioness ready to pounce.

Miss Breen's plea was in vain. With one backhand swipe from Kitty, the hefty schoolmarm practically flew across the road, landing in a pile of nettles, nose gushing like a crimson fountain. "Now, Miss Breen, let that be a lesson to you. That's how it feels to be slapped by someone stronger than you are. Never lay a hand on one of my children again. Do you understand me?"

"Yes, Mrs. Hogan. Oh, for the love of God, please…It was just a misunderstanding. It'll never happen again. You have lovely girls. All so bright…"

"Thank you, Miss Breen. I'm glad you approve of them. If they give you any trouble, just let me know. I'll deal with them myself. I discipline my children, not you. Your job is to educate them. Don't you agree?"

"Yes, yes...of course. We all have a job to do. Thank you, Kitty...I mean, Mrs. Hogan."

"You're most welcome, Brigid. Safe home, now."

The other episode that had puzzled and frightened Myles was the exchange he'd overheard between his mother and the Hannigan twins two years before. Billy and Bobby Hannigan were neighbors. They worked the big family farm and general store in Newtown, just off the Dublin Road, near Sally Gap. They were tall, burly redheads, popular with the girls and well-liked by one and all. Both were gifted football players, dominating defenders for the senior Wicklow team. They came from a well-respected family. Their father (Sean the Gap, as he was affectionately known) was a feared and famous IRA guerilla fighter. The twins seldom visited Rathdargan, so it was a surprise to hear their voices downstairs speaking in hushed tones with his mother early one Friday morning as Myles was waking.

Billy Hannigan, in his distinctive tenor voice, was speaking softly as Myles came fully awake.

"With all due respect, Mrs. Hogan, what we do or don't do with girls at the dances, that's our own business. I don't see where ya get off summoning us here to lecture us about Molly Redmond or what happened at the dance in Kilkenny Sunday night. If she has a complaint about anyt'ing, she should call the garda."

Kitty's voice, calm and deadly, came back—the same tone Myles had heard her use with Miss Breen. He felt a tightening in his stomach and fought back a wave of nausea. Suddenly, he felt sorry for the Hannigan twins and had to resist an impulse to rush downstairs and warn them.

His mother's voice continued the deadly inquisition.

"That's a good speech, Billy. It shows courage, which is admirable, given your situation. Now, Bobby, what do you have to say for yourself?"

"Not a t'ing, Mrs. Hogan, except that I'm sorry it had to come to this. Tell ya the God's honest truth, we didn't mean no harm. We had a few pints, an' t'ings got a bit out of hand, I s'pose. An' the reason we're here is 'cuz me father has great respect for you an' what ya did for the cause. We all have. We meant no harm, as God is my witness, Mrs. Hogan."

"Very good, Bobby. God is your witness, always has been and always will be, but we won't need to call on Him just yet. Your brother should take a page from your book, since contrition is the gateway to redemption. But you're both whistling past the graveyard if you think this is like going to confession and getting absolution.

"No. That won't do at all. Not this time. Here's why: I've known Molly Redmond since she was a little baby. Her mother and I were in the movement together long before you lads were even a gleam in your Daddy's eye. She's a lovely girl, and it so happens I'm her godmother—not that you should know that.

"So after the dance last Sunday night, she came by for our little chat, as usual. Only this time, she was hysterical. She told me everything. Everything. About what you blackguards did to her in Kelly's hayshed—or tried to do, I should say. I'm glad you have a few scruples left. Since her mother died in that ferry accident, I'm the one she turns to for advice. Thank God she did. And that's your bad luck…"

The long, ominous silence that followed was finally broken by Billy Hannigan's blustery voice.

"Look here, Mrs. Hogan, like I said, we came over here 'cuz Da respects you—we do, too, don't get me wrong—but what do ya want from us? Molly is no saint; she's a bit of a tayser—if you ask me. So I don't know what you want from us. What's done is done. It won't happen again, I can assure you of that. Is that the sort of t'ing ya want us to say?"

Upstairs, Myles had moved a little closer to hear his mother's reply. He could see her pacing back and forth through the cracks in the floorboards.

"Oh, I know it won't happen again. That's not what I'm worried about. No, not a whit. But, as I said, it's not going to be as simple as assuring me of your noble intentions. The road to hell is paved with those, as the fella says. Your amends will be much more tangible than mere words. As a show of good faith, I want three hundred pounds in twenty pound notes for Molly's education, with a written explanation to her that this is your way of apologizing to her and her family for the emotional distress you caused. Be sure you both sign your names , with Sean, your da, signing as witness. I also want you to donate one of your best Jersey cows to Pete Redmond to make up for the one that got killed on Dundrum Road last month. It was the only one they had. It's only a neighborly thing to do anyway; I'm sure your da won't mind.

"Oh, and while you're at it, it would be grand if you cut out five Cheviot ewe lambs and donated them, too. The Redmonds have had a couple of bad years and need a bit of sun to shine their way. You'll never even notice, but it'll make a world of difference to them."

Whatever had happened downstairs, the Hannigan twins went mute. Not a word of protest was spoken as Myles heard their hobnailed boots scrape the concrete kitchen floor.

"Right so, I see you boys understand me. Much better than calling the garda, wouldn't ya say? I'll see you at eight sharp tomorrow. Oh, if for any reason you don't make it, I'll be up by noon for a little conference with himself. Yer father and I go back a long ways, as you know."

Billy Hannigan was back the next morning at eight sharp, just as Kitty had ordained. He did not come in, but after a quiet conversation at the kitchen door, he walked slowly out of the farmyard. Myles watched him from the upstairs window, red curls flowing over his collar, as he closed the iron gate and walked slowly up the laneway. Even now, Myles remembered his mother's last words, in that menacing "Miss Breen" voice:

"Don't thank me. Always knew the Hannigans would rise to the occasion. Say hello to your parents for me and tell them there are no hard feelings here. I'm sure the Redmonds won't be pressing charges. That's the kind of thing that can ruin a young man's life. None of us would want that to happen, especially to a Hannigan. Safe home, now, Billy."

Myles recalled his visceral relief at what he saw as a reprieve for the Hannigans. He'd feared the worst for them, like Miss Breen. But they were men, of course. It was different. He couldn't imagine what they'd done to Molly Redmond to make his mother so mad—maybe pulled her hair or tried to kiss her—but he was glad it was over and done with. It still rankled him that this whole village seemed to know something about his mother that he did not. One thing was sure—it struck the fear of God into them. That part was a comfort to Myles; some people deserved to be afraid. Fear was the only thing they understood, like some of the brutal mountain boys at school. But it also scared him, for reasons he could not explain. And he was sick of being called

"Young Hogan of Rathdargan." He longed for an identity that he, Myles, could call his own.

He was also weary of hearing the depressing details of his father's neglect of his family dredged up and embellished, year after year. It was a story the whole community seemed to delight in telling and retelling, with each recitation a little less credible, a little more vicious.

How Jack missed his birth—as he did for all but one of his eight children born in their two-roomed farmhouse—and came home just in time to find his only son a cadaverous cluster of skin and bones, slumped in a coma. This rare visit had come in October, 1943, as the winter winds were returning to their ghostly antics, herding leaves from the giant oaks into every corner and crevice of the desolate farmyard.

A robust infant, Myles had lost half his body weight to a twin epidemic of whooping cough and German measles that had ravaged thousands of children across Europe. Myles's blonde three-year-old sister, Sheila, had suffocated in Kitty's arms. The local doctor—an alcoholic who practiced without a license—had prescribed baking soda.

Kitty just had to pray and wait "for God to take her," as she told Myles one chilly afternoon years later by the turf fire, where Kitty often surprised him with her reflections and admissions. Father Cavanagh, the parish priest in Enniskerry, was two days late coming to offer last rites and condolences. Uncle Patrick, Kitty's alcoholic brother, had been charged with the job of fetching the priest, but went to Dalton's Pub instead and forgot.

People never seemed to tire of telling how his penny-pinching uncle Mike—Kitty's grand uncle—had insisted that the undertaker delay closing Sheila's tiny white coffin should Myles expire and join her in it. (After three days, when Myles seemed to be hanging on, they went ahead with the burial.) True to form, Uncle Mike was calculating the cost of another coffin, and Jack missed Sheila's funeral.

But he arrived in time to save Myles's life. Or so the legend went. He'd heard of Kitty's predicament through the grapevine in Birmingham, where he worked on the line at Austin Motor Works. There was talk of a special type of paraffin lamp that worked magic in bringing relief to children stricken by the epidemic. Jack claimed he'd bought one for the family as soon as he got word. It was too late for Sheila, but for Myles, it worked: he got immediate relief and came out of his coma within hours of his father's homecoming.

As far as Myles was concerned, he never believed the heroic rescue story. It just didn't fit the man he'd come to believe his father to be. It seemed just another example of Jack Hogan getting off the hook. If it had been true, why did he leave them the next morning, without a word of goodbye, without leaving Kitty a single penny, or even his boarding house address? He simply walked out and left her to cope with her grief, to face the bleak winter with a house full of children and an empty cupboard.

Myles knew the real story, much less noble; he'd pieced it together from snippets of gossip he wasn't supposed to hear. Jack had lost his shirt gambling on "the nags" and had abandoned his family when Jim Dalton and Pete Coady—the local publicans—began to deny him credit for his belligerent binges, tolerated as long as he sang and paid for every round.

Jack's comings and goings were never quite clear to Myles. As far as he could tell, Jack first abandoned Kitty and their six daughters in February of 1937, five years before Myles was born. That time, he'd stayed away for two years, and then only came home to dodge the WWII draft. He'd stayed for three years, then vanished again in February of 1942, two months before Myles was born.

After that fleeting visit for Sheila's funeral in the fall of 1943, Jack went missing again, this time for keeps, it seemed. Other fathers who had to work in England came home every Christmas, Easter, and for the summer holidays. But not Jack Hogan. While his friends proudly displayed their visiting das at midnight mass, Myles meekly followed his mother as she marched to the front of Enniskerry Chapel with her brood of six to claim the family pew. No husband. No word. No hope.

Until now.

As word of Jack's heralded homecoming spread, the story of his departure gained new life. The neighbors warmed to the gossip, trumping Kitty's romantic renditions of Jack's adventures with details of their own.

"Now, when was it that Jack left again...?"

"Did he sell the bay mare to Father O'Meara—or was that the black stallion he'd won with at Gowran?"

They recited and embellished every painful detail of the deception.

How he'd lied about taking the mare to Foley's blacksmith's shop. Joe Foley told Kitty the shoes had never been fitted. They relived the story of how he'd sold the last brood mare, Dolly, before jumping the ferry to Holyhead, then on to Birmingham.

That Jack Hogan. What a character! Never a dull moment when he was around. It hasn't been the same since...

Myles heard from others how his mother had first got news of Jack—over a year later—and then only because he was accidentally spotted by a cousin who attended a concert in Shrewsbury, England, on a Saturday night. And there was Jack Hogan, in fine voice, center stage.

"Ah, what a wonderful tenor voice he had...Myles, sure some a dat talent musta rubbed off from yer father. Can you sing 'Slievenamon'? It was one of his favorites..."

There were times when Myles really hated him, with a burning, vengeful, damn-you-to-hell hatred. He was baffled by his mother's loyalty to her elusive husband. He hated how the locals kept reminding him of what a great hero his father was in the IRA as captain of the fabled "flying columns" and their daring assaults on the British occupation forces. Myles particularly resented the constant, invidious comparisons—whether in sports, singing, dancing, or work. "Sure, yer all right, but you'll never be as good as yer father. He was a great man for the football. Do you play...?"

More complicated was Myles's constant awareness of missing—not the flesh and blood man who was Jack Hogan—but the *idea* of a father and what he saw his friends enjoying with their das—hurling, boxing, football, prideful glances, tender touches to soothe the bumps and bruises. At such times, Myles longed for his da to be around, but it was a fleeting emotion—like dreams of winning the Irish Sweepstakes or owning his own team of Arabian horses.

After twelve years without so much as a single visit—Jack was a mere ferry ride away—Myles had given up, hardening his heart to the notion. The only sign of life he saw from his father over the years was the annual abusive letter pressuring Kitty to sell the farm. No money, not even a pound note; just a rant about how she'd always held him back with her lack of trust. Sneaking a peek at those missives, Myles could scarcely believe his eyes.

She'd once confided, in one of her fireside reflections, that the letters began in the aftermath of Jack's concerted efforts, against Irish law, to sell Rathdargan farm "out from under her"—without her permission, which he knew she would never give.

After getting one of these letters, Kitty cried for days, trying to hide her heartbreak behind red, swollen eyes. "I have such a problem with the pollen this year," she'd offer, fooling no one.

For all of that, there were still times when Myles tried to will the father of his dreams into existence. One specific incident stood out in his memory. He was about nine at the time. It was fox hunting season. The local hunters found him indispensable for one reason: The Hogan's had a terrific little fox terrier, named Nell, a white-and-tan sparkplug with classic markings.

Nell was famous for her ferocity and skill at flushing foxes from their dens—or dragging them out, if they were so foolish as to take her on. During the hunting season, there was a hunt every Sunday, and Nell was Myles's front-row ticket to the action. He was proud to be able to tag along, though it was dangerous; loaded shotguns in every hand. He was not even allowed to hold, let alone shoot, the old single-barreled shotgun that hung from its rack at the head of the stairs.

Myles knew it was Nell the hunters wanted; he was along as baggage, resented by some of the hunters for slowing them down. On this particular Sunday afternoon, the hunting party was in hot pursuit when they encountered a fast-running brook, three feet deep and four wide. The fox and dogs cleared the brook with no effort. Impatient fathers boosted their own sons over the stream, but, in their haste, forgot about Myles.

He remembered standing on the bank, crying, praying to Saint Anthony—patron saint of lost things—for his father to appear. When he didn't, Myles cursed St. Anthony for letting him down. "The curse a God on you, St. Anthony. Ya never come through when I need ya. An' I'm never going to ask you for another favor as long as I live. Ya can go to hell." He recalled his other grievances against St. Anthony when the stakes were high, like the time he'd lost his only hurling ball in the thick brambles behind the barn.

Eventually, Myles found a low spot downstream and waded across. But by the time he caught up with the hunt, he was soaked, bleeding from thorn bushes, and sobbing. No one even noticed that he'd been missing. Nell had the fox cornered, and her distinctive growls were punctuated by sharp yelps, meaning she was in trouble. It was only when Myles called her off that the hunters paid attention.

Saving Nell from the likely carnage of a cornered vixen meant spoiling their fun. "Sure, we were getting along fine until ya came along and ruined it. Maybe next time we'll just bring the dog…"

Jack Hogan came home to Rathdargan on May Day, 1958. It was a perfect spring day, rare in the moody Western Atlantic. It dawned sunny and cloudless, and, for once, never broke. May, Ireland's greenest month, had once again delivered its bounty.

The upper fields, next to Carrigoona Commons, were ablaze with daisies, their tiny white and yellow flowers forming the magic carpet dreamed of all winter. Daffodils, lilies, and forget-me-nots danced in the gentle breeze, blending their fragrance with the massive lilac hedge that formed a purple canopy over the handcrafted iron gateway to the farmhouse.

Birdsong echoed across the valley. The swallows were back— a welcome sign of spring—to reclaim their nests in the eaves of the cowshed. It was an idyllic setting to celebrate a family reunion.

Myles was like a jack-in-the-box at school that day, and was chastised repeatedly by Miss Breen, who found his conduct out of character. Having skipped two grades, he was one of her favorites, and she expressed her disappointment in no uncertain terms. Others, for the same transgression, would have been dealt six lashes of the dreaded "rod"—a mountain ash plant about two feet long. A standard teaching tool, used more than the atlas or textbook.

In Myles's case, Miss Breen had her reasons to show restraint. Besides, she genuinely liked and approved of Myles; just not today. "I must say that I find your conduct most unbecoming. Whatever has gotten into you, Myles Hogan? Very disappointing. I'm going to think twice about further privileges for you to go fetch you-know-what." This was her reference to Myles's perk of fetching her cache of jelly-filled doughnuts from Coady's grocery. She gave Myles one for his labor; it was their secret. But everyone knew of Miss Breen's weakness for doughnuts; it was hard to hide with her sixteen-stone waddle. And Myles's pals at school razzed him mercilessly for being "teacher's piggy pet."

Myles bolted from school at the clang of bell, taking the shortcut across Carrigoona Commons. Normally, he dawdled, taking at least two hours to cover the two miles. Pickup hurling games, a fistfight to kill the boredom, skinny-dipping at Powerscourt waterfalls—all offered distractions on the journey. This day, he was home in no time, determined to finish weeding his patch of the vegetable garden. He wanted to leave no room for Jack's famous fault finding, which Kitty inadvertently taught him to dread. "Wait till your father comes home. He won't put up with that..."

The mere thought of these encounters infuriated Myles. "Who the hell is he to tell me about my duties? Hadn't he neglected his for twelve years running? And haven't I done fine without him all these years? And what about Mammie? Sure, she'll just become sad, again, as she always has whenever his name is mentioned. And he'll just leave us again, anyway. Maybe I can just wait him out."

In the midst of elaborate preparations, Kitty had been on the lookout all afternoon. As Myles did when his sisters came home from nursing school, he watched for Ted Flanagan's Vauxhall—the only taxi in Enniskerry—to appear on the Carrigoona Road, which he could see for miles from his perch on the Rathdargin ridge.

Kitty wore a bright yellow dress with a brown belt—an outfit Myles had never seen before—and her dark, curly hair blew in the breeze. He'd never seen her look so beautiful, or so happy—smiling and laughing at things that weren't even funny. He guessed she was practicing her new routine.

Five-eight in her bare feet, with a strong, athletic figure, Kitty knew how to make the most of her elegant good looks. This day, she wore nylons and high heels that invited disaster on the farm-yard cobblestones. The four surviving girls were away at nursing school, so the welcoming party was down to Myles and his mother.

Hour after hour, he watched the Dundrum Road. Most of the cars just kept going, not making that right-hand turn at the crossroads for Rathdargan. Finally, after hours of lookout duty, he spotted Flanagan's Vauxhall. It turned right. Knowing it had to be Jack, he sounded the alarm: "Here he comes! They just turned at Doyle's Cross."

With the alert, Kitty went charging toward the lilac canopy, running the full two hundred yards of winding, sycamore lane-way, uphill in her high heels. In that moment of euphoria, of hope against hope, all was forgiven: the abandonment, the drunken abuse, the deceptions and neglect. Once again, Jack

Hogan was being given a hero's welcome; Kitty's faithful heart greeted him as any loving husband coming home from a normal, essential, bread-winning trip.

Myles couldn't stand it; he refused to join the parade. He expected to be coaxed, as usual, but Kitty hadn't even noticed his absence. He sat on the front steps, brooding, while Kitty and the border collies rushed to greet the prodigal father. By the time they emerged jubilantly through the gateway next to the farmhouse—thirty yards away—Myles had arrived at a plan of action.

His parents strode forward as if in a wedding parade. Kitty had both of her arms locked around Jack's trim waist. Myles saw his matter-of-fact mother clinging to this stranger with a distant, dreamy look he'd never seen before. It was as if Jack had never left, as if the cover story had been true all along, and this loyal provider had just gone to the forge to have the mare shod.

Jack's white cotton shirt billowed in the wind and he carried a battered tan suitcase. He was tall and handsome, just as people had been telling Myles all his life. What if he'd been wrong? What if the stories were all true? Jack was laughing, full of life and basking in the glow of Kitty's adoration. They looked like a couple right out of *Failte* magazine, out for a stroll in the lush Wicklow countryside.

Kitty was cheerfully explaining why Myles hadn't been with the welcoming party at the road gate. Apparently, he was shy. Finally, with an abrupt change of tone, she turned toward Myles and issued one of her sharp commands: "Myles, come meet your father, right now!"

Myles stood up and walked slowly toward the stranger, working hard not to betray the terror he felt at what he was about to do. He felt his big, bold plan dissolve with each step, like a slow leak in his bike tire. They met about halfway to the farmhouse, just above the open spring well. The trickling of the running spout in the yard suddenly grew noisy. Myles had to stifle an urge to turn and run.

Their eyes met for the first time, father and son, searching, like boxers in an opening round. No trust; animal suspicion. Myles noticed his father had the same deep blue eyes and dimpled cheeks as himself. Now those older eyes twinkled with mischief, as if Jack was about to tell a hilarious joke.

He smiled at Myles conspiratorially, then reached in his pocket with crowd-pleasing deliberation, saying to no one in particular, "So this is my great big son. I brought you something I think you're gonna like..." With great flourish, he pulled out a gorgeous silver watch, a fashionable Timex. It had a chain about a foot long, with a silver T-buckle on the end. He held it high for all to admire, then lowered it into Myles's outstretched palm.

Without a word, Myles took the watch, gazed at it for a long few seconds, then threw it with all the force he could muster straight at his father's head, yelling: "I don't want yer watch! I don't want anythin' from ya! I wish ya'd just stay away from us..."

He didn't wait to see where the watch landed—just tore down the laneway toward his refuge, the garden, vaguely registering over his shoulder the flurry of apologies from his mother. "He's not like this at all. I don't know what got into him. Oh, Jack, please don't be upset. I'll talk with him...He'll apologize...I'm so sorry...I had no idea..."

Myles had learned from watching Kitty over the years that the best balm for upset is hard work. Now he threw himself into weeding the lettuce ridges, his head down, his back to the house, where he could hear the subdued voices of his parents. Then he heard footsteps on the garden path. Kitty was coming to reprimand him, to order him to apologize. He didn't turn around, just kept working, bracing for the verbal assault.

It never came. To his surprise, it was his father's voice that broke the silence: "This is a beautiful garden you've grown here, son. So clean. I used to plant lettuce and onions in this very same spot when I was your age. It's the sunniest place in the whole orchard. Did you know we used to call this 'the orchard'? The field over the house used to be filled with apple trees—people would come from all over to pick them. The trees would be in full bloom right about now—all shades of pink and white. We had such great yield, we just gave them away for free. The cattle and pigs ate the rest."

He kept up the monologue, squatting down in the row beside Myles in his polished shoes and white shirt, moving with him up the row. This went on for at least a half hour, during which time Myles kept working, but never looked at his father or said a word. The speaker might as well have been invisible. Finally, Jack stood up, dusted off his pants, and mumbled something about needing to wash up for dinner before vanishing behind the orchard wall.

Myles waited till he heard the wooden gate close behind him, then broke into tears of confused rage that watered the fledgling lettuce plants, lasting till he finished the row, exhausted and afraid of facing his mother.

At last, Kitty emerged, under the guise of picking scallions and lettuce for supper. To his surprised relief, she assured him that she was not upset, that she understood it would take time for him to get used "to having a man around the house."

It was the last thing he needed to hear. His anger returned, surprising both of them: "I'm never gonna get used to it. We were doin' fine without 'im. And I'm not goin to call 'im Da either, an' there's no use trying ta make me."

"All right, a Cushla, I know this is hard for you. But I still expect you to show your manners and to be polite. There's no excuse for rudeness. Promise me that you won't let us down. Do this for me, please!"

Myles dug at his tear-stained face with two muddy fists, promised her without conviction, and went in to wash up for dinner. He was used to being without a father, but now it was beginning to look like he was also about to lose his mother, too—at least the one he'd known up to now. Fine, maybe he'd just run away to England; that would show her about a "man in the house." He could find work on the buildings; four of his cousins had already gone to Sheffield, and they were only a few years older.

But Jack Hogan would prove hard to resist; he had a magic about him that Myles felt drawn to. Even mundane tasks like shearing sheep or clipping the pony became occasions of performance and celebration. Everyone—men, women, and children—even the animals seemed to vie for his attention. He was charming, entertaining, and loved to make people laugh.

Myles knew his father had won several singing competitions, both in Ireland and England, but he had no idea what that meant. Then, on his second night home, Myles came to understand why Jack Hogan was known as "The Voice."

With plenty of Guinness being passed around, conversations buzzing in the kitchen, the usual suspects had arrived to perform their party pieces. No one was paying much attention—everyone talking at once—until someone shouted, "Hush up! Jack is goin' ta sing."

As if someone has hit a master switch, the house instantly falls silent. Jack stands up, steps confidently to the middle of the room, takes a deep breath, and launches.

His selection is Thomas Moore's classic, "She Is Far from the Land," a song familiar to all.

From the first line, all Myles's resentments and plots for escape dissolve. His father's voice is unlike anything he's ever heard—sweet, enchanting, and almost like a musical instrument in its perfection. Like the rest of the audience, Myles finds himself swept up in the emotion of the moment, crushed by the grief, still embracing it with both ecstasy and anguish that he has never experienced with other singers. By the end of the first verse, several people, women and men, are openly weeping. Some are actually sobbing, shoulders heaving. Handkerchiefs are out, arms clasping shoulders in comfort, and Myles finds himself crying openly with the others, without self-consciousness.

The words, poetry sung from the heart, etched themselves in Myles's memory, words he would recite and sing in faraway places decades later:

> *She is far from the land where her young hero sleeps,*
> *And lovers are round her, sighing:*
> *But coldly she turns from their gaze, and weeps,*
> *For her heart in his grave is lying!*

In full performance persona, Jack swings toward the kitchen audience he'd had his back to for the first verse. His hands form a moving circle in front of him as he sings, making deliberate and lingering eye contact with each person as he delivers the next lines:

> *She sings the wild song of her dear native plains,*
> *Every note which he loved awaking;*
> *Ah! little they think who delight in her strains,*
> *How the heart of the Minstrel is breaking!*

He had lived for his love, for his country he died,
They were all that to life had entwined him,
Nor soon shall the tears of his country be dried,
Nor long will his love stay behind him.

For the finale, he comes full circle, pauses for several seconds, then turns toward the finish. The silence is perfect as he hits the pièce de résistance.

Oh! Make her a grave, where the sunbeams rest,
When they promise a glorious morrow;
They'll shine o'er her sleep, like a smile from the West,
From her own loved island of sorrow!

As Jack finishes on a caressing inflection of "sorrow," his audience sits stock still, mesmerized. Then come the tears, mingled with self-conscious giggles. The applause is long and loud, everyone on their feet, even Mick Murphy, who never rises unless to relieve himself or to go home. They are uniformly awe-stricken. Shouts of "No trouble taya, Jack! More! More!—Give us 'The Foggy Dew,'" can be heard in the adjoining townsland.

Jack obliges, without coaxing, leading off with the "The Foggy Dew," then "Dawning of the Day," "If I Were a Blackbird," closing with a nationalist favorite, "The Croppy Boy." He delivers his medley of ballads with the same fluid energy, the beautiful voice, the engaging presence. Long before the final song, Myles has been captured by his father's magnetic field, holding onto his jacket, proud to claim him as his very own da.

The ramblers notice the gesture and applaud that, too, long and loud. In the background, Myles can see Kitty, beaming her approval as she busies herself with the tea.

The spring and summer flew by in blur of manly activity. Myles spent hours with his da, just the two of them, working on blocked drains, collapsed fences, and overgrown hedges. Sometimes they just wandered around the farm, like two pals, taking stock of the dilapidation, while Jack displayed the same comedic skills of their aging neighbor, Andy Murphy—mimicry, jokes, foibles, legends—all in a day's work.

Jack seemed to have lots of money, spent it freely, and was in no hurry to find work outside the farm or new ways to provide for the family. No one questioned the source of his largesse. Irishmen often came home from England feeling flush and spending lavishly, even if they couldn't afford it. After all, Jack had been gone for over a decade and might have changed his ways. Rumor had it that he'd won the lottery in Birmingham. Another had it that he had a recording contract with Decca Records and had been given a big advance. Sure, wasn't he…"A finer tenor than John McCormick!"

More remarkable still, he never touched a drop of drink all summer. Given the man's reputation, that was nothing short of a miracle. Jack brushed it off with a simple comment that drink "doesn't agree with me anymore" when pressed with "sure, one bottle of stout won't kill ya."

Some days, instead of farm projects, they went hunting down in the lower meadows. At last, Myles had his chance to do what he'd been dreaming about for years: show off Nell's skills and his own knowledge of game and fox habitat to his da. In turn, Jack taught him how to shoot the ancient single-barreled shotgun that had hung unused in the upstairs rafters. Kitty had warned Myles against the dire consequences of even touching the gun, though he sometimes sneaked in and played war games, pretending he was an IRA marksman, killing scores of British soldiers as they came swarming across Sugarloaf Mountain.

That was before Jack came home. Now he was allowed to take target practice openly in the orchard, using a thick wedge of oak nailed to an apple tree as a bull's-eye. Once he got used to the violent kick of the butt against his jaw—which knocked him flat the first time he pulled the trigger—he showed a lightning speed and accuracy that drew praise from all quarters. Soon Myles was bagging pheasant and rabbits weekly, beating his father to the mark after the dogs flushed the game from the furze.

It was on one of those hunting expeditions that Myles came to know another side of his father. He also learned a well-kept secret about his mother that cast her in a whole new light. The conversation began after Myles had downed a pheasant with a good shot, and Jack, sensing his son morphing into a man, opened a delicate subject: his years in the IRA.

"You know son, the crack of a gun always reminds me of when I led the Flying Column down in Bunclody back in '19. We'd been tracking the Black n' Tans for a week after they burned out the whole village of Kiltealy. Well, we hit 'em at three in the mornin'. Blew up the barracks where they were billeted, out toward Vinegar Hill. Never knew what hit 'em. Bastard foreign riff-raff...Criminal element turned loose from British prisons and armed on condition they come over an' massacre us. Five of 'em escaped the first blast, but we blew their balls off as they came charging out of the back."

"What happened after that, Da?"

"They caught us in Enniscorthy four months later, but not before we'd done several more jobs like that."

"How come they didn't kill you like they did when they caught Padraig Pearse and the others in the Easter Rising?"

"Did yer mother never tell ya the story? Sure, I'm not surprised; it's not like her to dwell on the past. Or to brag."

Myles was now listening to an entirely different man than he'd known before. Gone was the funny raconteur. In his place was a soldier, focused and gleaming at the memory of battle. This was the real IRA hero, the one he'd never believed existed. Yet, here he was listening to the firsthand account, like a dream come to life. Myles sank down on the stone wall, ready to drink it all in, watching his father's glistening blue eyes harden as he warmed to the story.

"Well, see, we were arrested and taken to the local jail in Enniscorthy. The whole county knew what happened; someone had informed on us, one of our own. We were to face the Tans' firing squad the following Wednesday. So here's what happens. We were allowed one last visit from family and friends to say our goodbyes. No men, only women. I was dating your mother at the time, sort of—she was Kitty Cusack then, a gorgeous slip of a girl, but secretly a commander in the local Cumann na mBan."

"I thought only the men could be commanders?"

"Oh, no, son. The women were commissioned, too. Kitty had a reputation—well-deserved, may I say—as a fierce Republican. Absolutely fearless. And deadly. She shows up on Tuesday night, acting the green, gawky country girl—'Sorry to bother ya, Sir'— with freshly baked brown bread, four packs of Sweet Afton fags, and guess what else?"

"A hacksaw blade?"

"Ha, you've been reading too many comics. No—a sawed-off shotgun—stowed under her big winter coat."

Jack smiled at the memory and lit his pipe, puffing to fill the silence. Myles felt his pulse race. His mother with a shotgun? Was this the same woman who forbade him to even handle the old shotgun gathering dust upstairs before his da came home? He watched Jack's face for a few more seconds, before asking, "So did she manage to hide the shotgun from the guards?"

Jack laughed and rolled on: "No, that was not the plan. She had a different idea. The guard, a Tanner, never knew what hit 'im; she fired at point blank range...blew a hole in him the size of yer fist."

Myles tried to swallow, but felt his mouth go dry and his chest tighten. Then he heard himself say in a faint voice that sounded high-pitched and distant, "You mean ta tell me that Mammie killed the guard...I mean, the Tanner?"

Jack smiled indulgently at the boy's amazement, continuing calmly, as though telling a bedtime story. He moved in closer to Myles, holding his gaze, warming to the subject, enjoying both the memory and the discomfiture of his audience.

"Oh, absolutely. Dead as a doornail. He made one fatal mistake—didn't think a country lass would have the nerve to pull the trigger; feckin' eejit dared her: 'Go ahead,' he sez, 'ya Fenian bitch. I dare ya. Ye don't got the fucken nerve.' Sure we all heard 'im yell it from up an' down the cell block. We knew they'd be the last words the Tanner ever spoke. Didn't know Kitty Cusack like the rest of us...That woman had nerves of steel, tougher than most of the lads in the movement. A better shot, too. Kitty always took care of business. Always got the job done."

With that, Jack looked off in the distance and paused to relight the pipe. A long silence followed before Myles broke in, choking back tears.

"I never knew any of that, Da. Mammie never told me...How could she? So how did you escape?"

Another long pause, puffs on the pipe, and a resigned sigh. "Well, after Kitty sprung us—all twelve of us...Oh, listen, 'tis a long story, son. We split up. Packie Hayden, Denny Brennan, an' me stayed together an' got out to Canada; ended up in Montreal. We had contacts and a lot of help up the chain of command. But that's why yer mother and I had to meet up in New York after it had all settled down years later.

"I'll tell ya the rest some other time. Sure, Mick Collins and I were best pals; started out as hand-picked lieutenants in the IRB—Irish Republican Brotherhood—before DeValera and The Treaty tore us all asunder. I can't bear to even think about the betrayals and treachery; all those fine young lads and lassies, tortured and martyred for...for what? Look what it got us."

The memory seemed to wilt him. Gone was the aloof story-teller, spinning a yarn. His soft tenor voice broke, and tears welled up in the blue eyes, turning gray in anguish. Embarrassed, he turned away, trying to regain his composure. "I'm sorry, son. I shouldn't have told you all this. Promise me ya won't tell yer mother I told you about Enniscorthy. I shoulda let sleeping dogs lie..."

"I promise, Da. I won't say a word."

With that, Jack stood up, stuffed the pipe in his pocket, and started up the hill toward the red-tiled farmhouse. They walked the distance in silence, deep in their own thoughts, Myles a few steps behind his father. His mind raced with questions and the dawning realization that his world had just been turned upside down.

Suddenly, the mysteries of deference to his mother made sense.

After each incident, Myles had assumed his mother, a naturally dominant personality, intimidated her targets with sheer force of will. Now, he understood the pitiful pleading, the sudden show of compassion, the ready admission of guilt. They all had one thing in common: terror. They weren't facing his mother; they were facing Kitty Cusack, legendary commander in the Cumann na mBan and secret enforcer for the IRA.

But did they know the whole truth? That she'd shot a Black an' Tan prison guard, and the only living witness was Jack Hogan? Maybe the whole truth was worse. Perhaps she'd shot others? If so, how many? And who besides Jack knew?

Myles was left to ponder these questions alone. He would have to bide his time before he could even broach the subject with his Da, and Kitty was completely off limits; on that front, he was sworn to secrecy.

After that one extraordinary tale of his jailbreak, Jack returned to his other persona: an endless fountain of hilarious mimicry, ancient wisdom, songs, and poetry. Myles, in turn, decided to focus on the bright side of this newly revealed heritage. He was the only son of Kitty Cusack and Jack Hogan, Cumann na mBan and IRA insurgents who'd trounced the Black 'n' Tans, hooligans and murderers all. This was nothing to be ashamed of. In fact, he was proud of his pedigree. After all, Kitty and Jack had put it all on the line for Irish freedom when it mattered most. He didn't know anyone else who could say that about *both* their parents.

So resolved, he got up each day now intent on making the most of being alone with his da. He never raised the topic of the IRA again, and Jack avoided all references to his days "on the run." Instead, they seemed to have reached a tacit agreement that Rathdargan farm would be their new cause.

Jack taught Myles the verses to all his favorite songs—*Slievenamon, the Croppy Boy, Dawning of the Day,* and Myles's favorite, *Kevin Barry.* They cleaned out the old car shed, built a workbench, and cut down several hardwood trees—ashes and oaks—for the new paddock they'd planned behind the stable.

At night, Hogan's farmhouse turned into a lively "rambling house"—the center of community fellowship and entertainment. Gone were the days of isolation when Myles and Kitty wouldn't see a soul from one Sunday to the next. The Voice had raised the ante; singers never heard from before emerged to perform and match their talent against Himself. The same with the music— and all the other performances, including the storytelling, poetry, and occasional tug-of-war on the long summer evenings. It was the best summer of Myles's life, far and away. He finally had a father of his own, and one who was supremely talented, great fun, and a genuine IRA hero to boot.

Then, one balmy August evening, their idyllic summer ended.

The ramblers had assembled for another night of music and storytelling, but Jack was still down in Enniskerry on some errand. Myles heard the border collies first, their barking chorus unusually shrill—with Parnell, the big black alpha, dropping into an ominous crouch, hackles up, sounding as if gearing up for mortal combat with some hapless foe. This was a sound Myles had never heard the borders make before, and he felt a shiver invade his whole body.

Kitty finally tuned in to the din in the farmyard and turned to Myles without noticing that he'd turned pale. "Myles, will you go out and call off those dogs! They're giving me a headache with all that randy-boo." When she saw his hesitation, she picked up the Tilly lamp and, without further comment, stormed into the dark farmyard to see what all the fuss was about. "Parnell! Shep! Rover! Come to heel! I said, HEEL!"

With that, the dogs went mute; but not quite. They stopped barking, but Parnell kept baring his fangs in his alpha snarl, while the others growled and refused to lie down as they normally would when Kitty took charge. As a pack, they paced back and forth, glaring toward the outer gate with baleful suspicion.

Standing just beyond the gate, frozen in fear, was a homely little woman, dressed in black with a large hat on top of a wizened little head. As she stepped into the farmyard, Myles could see her large pair of glasses reflect the light as she introduced herself as Fanny Wilcox, explaining that Ted Flanagan had driven her up from Enniskerry, but had to go for another fare, leaving her to carry her large suitcase down the long driveway by herself. She looked exhausted, leaning on a cane, and Kitty immediately felt sorry for her. "Well, come on in and have a cup of tea and some refreshments, Fanny. You look famished, and sure , who wouldn't be after lugging that suitcase down the lane all by yourself. I'm surprised at Ted to leave a woman in such a lurch. Shame on him."

Fanny waved this aside with, "No, no—Ted seemed like a nice chap, really. Very polite and friendly, 'e was. I don't want to put you to any trouble, but I'm looking for Paddy Hogan, and I understand 'e lives 'ere." Here was an accent Myles had never heard, and he could barely make out a word.

"I'm afraid you may have the wrong farm, Fanny. This is Jack Hogan's house, and he's away at the moment, but we don't know any Paddy Hogan."

Fanny sipped her tea, glanced through her horn-rimmed glasses at the assembled ramblers, and Myles, before speaking. Then, with a condescending cackle and an air of conspiracy, she leaned toward Kitty and whispered, "You may want to 'ear the rest of wot I 'ave to say privately. Can we go into another room, then?" Caught off guard, Kitty blushed and said, "Of course, of course…sure let's go up to the parlor so that we can talk. Myles will join us." Myles moved past the ramblers toward the parlor, but as he walked by Fanny, he felt her cold, clawlike hand grasp his wrist and whisper, so that all could hear, "I don't think we want our knuck here listening to wot I 'ave to say." Kitty recognized the British taunt: knuck—dimwit, eejit—but hadn't heard it since her days as a nursemaid in London, when it was used to ridicule Irish country girls—fresh off the boat—on the "downstairs" staff of her upper-crust employer.

Ignoring Fanny, she guided Myles in front of her as the three of them withdrew to the parlor—the formal room reserved for company—to the gawking silence of the ramblers. Kitty poured more tea and invited Fanny to proceed, which she did with an air of being in a deep conversation with a long-lost friend. Her story, which took over an hour to tell in her halting, Yorkshire style, erased all doubt of its credibility.

"Paddy came to live at Windgate House about five years ago. I'd been running the boarding house ever since me 'usband died in WWII, rest his soul. He was a career military man, you see, Captain Wilcox. A good man; a good provider. Paddy and I grew very fond of each other, and got engaged a year ago. He told me all about 'is life—about Rathdargan farm, about 'aving a sister wi' six children—five daughters and a boy—who'd lost her 'usband in the war, just like me. He told me how he was helping her out, letting 'er stay 'ere, though 'e was legal owner of the farm. But 'e was allowing his sister—ye—to live 'ere out of kindness—not cuz 'e had to, mind you. And 'e always did say how 'e intended to come back to Ireland to run the farm when the time was right.

"Being 'is fiancée, I trusted 'im with my life's savings, five hundred pounds, which 'e said 'e needed to fix up Kildargan, till 'e could send for me. I was planning on selling Windgate House as a going concern—I'm tired of all the 'eadaches that go with running a boarding 'ouse. You 'ave no idea wot goes on."

Myles looked at Kitty as the story ended. The only sound in the parlor was the loud ticking of the grandfather clock by the heavy mantelpiece, over which hung stern portraits of Hogan ancestors across the generations. Outside, the border collies were still barking in their high-pitched chorus, and Parnell, the alpha, was pacing back and forth, still growling, disturbed by something unseen in the summer night.

From Fanny's account, there was no doubt that "Paddy" was Jack, up to his old tricks. As always, they'd caught up to him, only this time with his wife and son as stricken witnesses and a gallery of ramblers to spread the gossip as fast as their legs could carry it.

Myles knew trouble when he saw it, and this had all the makings. He looked at the intruder with unvarnished hostility. Fanny Wilcox had not been granted her fair share of nature's bounty. In fact, she was one of the ugliest people Myles had ever laid eyes on; more detached observers would readily agree. Under five feet and somewhat obese, she walked with a bow-legged limp, and had one glass eye that looked dead, almost amphibian. To cap it off, she spoke in a high-pitched Yorkshire dialect, "Gur blimey, a rum lot, eh wot?"—as enervating to the Celtic ear as fingernails on a blackboard.

To Myles's amazement, Kitty finished her tea with elaborate politeness, then invited Mrs. Wilcox to stay: "Just for the night." But Myles was having none of it. "Mammie, I don't believe a word of what she's saying. How do we know she's telling the truth? And why can't we wait till Da comes home? Besides, where is she going to sleep? We don't have any room for visitors, unless she wants to sleep in the hayshed." He said all this while glaring at Mrs. Wilcox and before Kitty had time to issue a reprimand. Embarrassed by his outburst, she now took control. "Myles Hogan, you will not talk to a guest like that. Apologize at once!" But Myles was in no mood to back down in front of this creature he sensed was up to no good. "I will not apologize. I haven't done anything to apologize for. But I'm going to see what Da has to say before I listen to one more word from either a yez." With that he bounded out of the parlor and made an elaborate display of stomping up the creaky wooden stairs.

Jack came home after all the ramblers had departed. It was quiet in the kitchen when he walked in to the unlovely presence of Fanny, sitting by the fire, teacup in hand. Caught red-handed, "Paddy" came clean and acknowledged that, yes, he and Fanny had "grown fond of each other." Myles, listening from the upstairs loft, couldn't believe his ears. He'd been wrong, and now his worst fears were being realized. This creature was going to stay here, which meant he would have to give up his room and sleep in the dark, dingy parlor on the lumpy old horsehair sofa.

There was one thing Myles didn't understand: his father's lack of taste. Surely, Myles thought, if his father was going to find another woman to "date," he could have picked someone who was at least presentable. Myles just couldn't imagine his handsome father being seen with Fanny Wilcox in public, or whatever else "being fond of" meant. When he mentioned this to his mother, she simply said, "Men will do strange things for drink, son. I hope you will never know what that's like."

The comment made no sense to Myles, but, watching his mother's mouth tighten, he let it go. But he vowed then and there that this ugly and evil creature had to go. He had no idea of how, but he knew he hated her and would stop at nothing to protect his family from this cackling menace.

Whatever was worked out by the adults, Mrs. Wilcox seemed in no hurry to leave. Whenever she went for one of her solitary walks around the farm, Myles could hear his parents fighting. First, his mother's voice raised in consternation; then, his father's usually soft tenor voice took on a hoarse, frightening harshness. Sometimes, too depressed to work, Myles would idle in the hayshed, leafing through a comic book, pretending to be busy. Terrified of losing his da again, he began to conjure up schemes to rid Rathdargan of Mrs. Wilcox.

This took little effort, for Fanny Wilcox—having always been childless—made no bones about her dislike for children, especially boys and Myles in particular. She kept on referring to him as "our knuck"—a phase he, fortunately, never understood—in her grating, screechy dialect. No one told her to knock off the obvious taunting. Later, she tried charming him, but soon gave up in the face of his silent disdain. Myles went out of his way to be rude, even refusing to be in the same room when she was present.

After a month of brooding hatred, he decided to kill Mrs. Wilcox. It soon became an obsession. At first, he felt guilty, pacing his room at night and imagining his confession to Father Cavanagh. After all, this would be murder, clearly a mortal sin. Fires of hell for eternity; no priest could even offer him absolution.

On the other hand, Mrs. Wilcox wasn't even a Catholic. She was barely human; some kind of Protestant. She was going to burn in hell anyway. Surely it was no sin to rid his family of this parasite; it'd be like killing a rat or shooting a cuckoo to keep it from preying on an innocent robin's nest. God would understand this, and so would Father Cavanagh.

Seizing on this line of thought, Myles felt relieved, free to focus on concrete plans.

His first idea was to follow Fanny on one of her walks and push her into one of the sinkholes near the far field where no one would ever find her. Myles had seen one of those quagmires swallow a two–thousand-pound cow; even eight strong farmers pulling on the end of a rope couldn't save her. He discarded the notion only once he remembered how slowly the cow sank; it had taken at least eight hours. He could imagine Fanny Wilcox, stuck and screaming in her shrill Yorkshire gibbberish so that the whole valley would be summoned to witness her accusations.

He finally settled on a concrete plan. It was as simple as it was vicious. He would invite Mrs. Wilcox to go hunting with him in the lower meadow, there would be an accident, and she wouldn't come back. He rehearsed his lines for the aftermath.

"I don't know, Mammie. It all happened so fast. Mrs. Wilcox wanted to learn to shoot, and I let her give it a go. The borders were barking, which startled her, then the gun backfired , and then she was laying there, the dogs surrounding her , barking like they'd gone mad...I'm really sorry. I shouldn't have let her use the gun. It's all my fault."

He imagined his mother and the neighbors trying to console him.

"Now, Myles, you shouldn't blame yourself. Mrs. Wilcox was a grown woman, capable of making a decision. I'm sure you were just trying to be nice to her. But I know this must be very hard for you."

It was now only a matter of how to get his quarry in the lower meadow on a different kind of hunting expedition. Never an athletic person, Mrs. Wilcox was not likely to jump at the chance to go hunting, but Myles was determined to convince her.

"Mrs. Wilcox, would you be interested in seeing where the pheasants lay their eggs in the Far Field?"

"Wot is this? A wildlife outin' being offered by our knuck? Well, well, well...Wonders never cease. An' I thought ye didn't like me very much. We'll see. Maybe when I'm feeling a little bet-tah. Not today, luv. Run along now."

"All right, Mrs. Wilcox, I could even teach you how to shoot rabbits and foxes. Might come in handy sometime if you're going to be around Kildargan."

"Well, it might, at that. I nevah thought a' that. Me, shootin'. Blimey! You 'ave some imagination for a young lad. I may have misjudged ye. I do believe I'll take ye up on it, soon as I'm feelin' a bit more chipper."

Myles smiled and shivered at the ease of his conquest. Now the question: Did he have the nerve to pull this off? He'd killed and seen killing before: Billy Flood butchering a hog; Packie Ryan shooting his old sheepdog, Ben; Peter Doyle putting down the bay colt with the broken leg. No one liked it; they just did what had to be done in the situation. This was no different, just something that had to be done. Another hard truth.

He carefully rehearsed each step until he had it down by heart. First have her handle the gun to get her fingerprints on it—all the detective comics made this point. Then teach her to aim it. Next, take the gun away in mock anger at her awkward-ness, start to walk away, turn around, aim, and fire at point-blank range. Easy. Like shooting a jackdaw on a fencepost.

For several weeks, as the days grew shorter, Myles began to panic, badgering Mrs. Wilcox about her promise to go hunting. She kept putting him off; it never seemed to be quite the right time. Maybe she was on to him; evil mind reading evil mind. He seldom slept for more than a couple of hours, and when he did, his dreams turned to nightmares of blood and gore from which he'd awake screaming. Even daylight brought no relief, his mind a chamber of horrors: Father Cavanagh's voice condemning him to hell; Mrs. Wilcox's mangled ghost at the window; Myles hanging from a scaffold at Mountjoy Gaol, body twisting in the wind.

He was cleaning out the cowshed when Jimmy Dunphy's high-pitched whistle sent the borders into their frenzied greeting. They knew Jimmy, but never ceased to greet him with full-throated barking, delighted at the chance to show off their guarding prowess. This time, Jimmy was lucky: Kitty was there to greet him with her steady smile, which faded once she saw the little green telegram in his arthritic fingers.

He went into his ritual delivery, which infuriated Kitty and destroyed any chance Jimmy had of being invited in for tea and scones. Myles came up from the shed at the sound of the borders, just in time to hear Jimmy plead, "Maybe I should wait in case you want to send word back." This time, Myles didn't say anything; he just gave Jimmy a hard stare as Kitty abruptly turned her back and trotted down the stairs, tripping over the borders as they swarmed with the excitement of the moment.

Halfway to the kitchen, Kitty pulled up and said, "Oh, my God, the telegram is for Fanny. Do you know where she is?" Myles had seen her go for her regular walk about an hour earlier, and he instinctively grabbed the telegram and ran in the direction he'd seen Mrs. Wilcox go.

He met her at the hazel corral, walking slowly toward the farmhouse, taking in the warmth of the sun as it rose from behind the Sugarloaf. She looked small and vulnerable, and, for a moment, Myles felt sorry for her and guilty of his wicked design on her life. Seeing him sprinting toward her, she immediately erased his guilt with, "Well, well…if it isn't our knuck, snooping around, are we?" Myles just stared at her in his practiced nonchalance, held up the telegram and said, "Mammie said this is for you. The postman just delivered it."

Fanny snatched the telegram from Myles's outstretched hand and slit the little green envelope with one sharp flick of her talon-like fingernail. Myles watched her as she read the brief message. After several seconds, she looked past him with her glass eye and muttered, "Oh, dear. I must go back at once. There's been a dreadful death at Windgate. Poor Peter Boyle, one of my boarders, has hanged hisself in the upstairs bathroom." With that she turned and trotted toward the farmhouse in her bandy-legged gait, puffing and panting, with Myles walking behind her at a fast clip to keep up.

Mrs. Wilcox quickly related her story to Kitty. Jack was out in the fields, fixing fences, and Myles ran down to tell him the news. He said nothing, just came back to the house, briefly spoke with Fanny, then grabbed Myles's bike and rode off to Enniskerry to fetch Ted Flanagan for Fanny's departure in the morning.

Next morning, as the sun's first rays edged across the Sugarloaf Range, Myles staggered downstairs to find Mrs. Wilcox packed, with Flanagan's green Vauxhall idling at the road gate. She begged Myles for a hug and, without hesitation, he clung to her and sobbed as though his heart was breaking.

"Wot's a mattah? Don't take on so. I didn't even think ya liked me...Blimey! Our knuck has a 'art after all."

"Bye, Mrs. Wilcox. Sorry we didn't have a chance to go hunting. Maybe some other time—if you ever come back."

"Aye, son. Maybe then. Between you n' me, that may be a while. I doubt I'll be back. But you can come stay wi' me in Birmingham. I know a lot a young ladies that'd like the cut a yer jib, if ya know wot I mean. Take care, lad. Yer not such a bad knuck, after all..."

The Hogans—all three of them—waved goodbye as Flanagan's taxi disappeared around the bend down the Wexford

Road. They walked back to the house in silence, like a funeral procession, each in a private turmoil they dared not speak of.

Something had died during Fanny's stay; intuitively, they all knew that the innocent laughter and family joy they'd known just a few weeks ago was gone forever. The only question for Myles was how he would get through the next few days without letting his relief, grief, and anger spill out all over the kitchen floor. What was he going to say to his da? To Mammie? To his pals in school? To the snooping neighbors?

Predictably, Jack took the line of least resistance: As soon as the green taxi was out of sight, he promptly changed his clothes, pumped up the bike tires, and muttered something about going to Borris to talk to Jimmy Doran about a horse. From the look on Kitty's face, Myles knew she didn't believe a word of it. They had no reason to trust him or believe a word he said. Myles could see some combination of disdain, worry, and alarm on his mother's face, and something else: a new look—one that he had never seen before.

No longer able to stand the furtive look on his father's face, Myles hastily dodged out to the hayshed to pursue his chores. From there, he could overhear his parents' voices, raised in anger. Kitty spoke first: "How do I know you're going Doran's? You always make up some cock n' bull story when all you're doing is goin' to the Joyce's pub. Or are you just going back with Fanny to Windgate? Why don't you just be man enough to tell me this time, not sneak off as usual?" Jack, his soft tenor now hoarse with anger: "I'll do whatever I feckin' well please, and no woman is going to tell me where I can come or go. I'm was goin' to Jimmy Doran's, but now I think I'll go straight to Joyce's. Why the hell not? Might as well be hung for a sheep as a lamb. It's all the same to the high and mighty Kitty Cusack. You can go straight to hell, woman, for all I care." Myles heard his mother mutter something unintelligible before they broke off , with his da slamming the kitchen door behind him and storming into the farmyard with his hat and coat on.

As Jack angrily wheeled the bike toward the road gate, the borders suddenly became excited and barked menacingly at his back, the way they did at departing strangers. Irritated at the ruckus, Jack wheeled on the closest border collie, Rover, and kicked him viciously in the ribcage. The young dog whined and ran toward Myles for comfort, as Jack slammed the gate behind him with a few muttered curses at the dogs.

That night—the first without their odd guest—the ramblers arrived at dusk, as usual, their expectations high. The borders kicked up their usual racket, but quickly settled down to enjoy the routine camaraderie. Mrs. Wilcox's presence had not damp-ened the rambler's spirits or concentration one bit. It would take more than her awkward attempts at participation to do that. In fact, they'd been more than gracious to her—Myles noted with some resentment.

He'd hoped for a show of support; instead, he'd become the target of the ramblers' pious lectures on the virtues of being polite and "not letting yer family down." That's a good one, Myles thought bitterly, I'm the one who's disgracing the family by not cozying up to this bow-legged creature from Birmingham?

When Jack was not home as the ramblers ambled in, the dis-appointment and curiosity was palpable. From the forced humor and the knowing looks, it was clear what they were thinking: the worst, the obvious, why not? Had that not been borne out since Fanny's arrival in August? Surely, there was no reason to assume things were suddenly going to be hunky-dory. They could barely restrain their winks when Kitty told them that "Himself" had only gone to Enniskerry to see Jimmy Doran. They knew better. The more Kitty reassured them, the more pity Myles could detect in their ruddy faces.

They knew all along the arrangement couldn't last, and while they felt sorry for Kitty and Myles, they felt even sorrier for themselves. Myles could see it in their sad faces, looking at the door as people filed in, staring past each familiar face to see if Jack might be among them. Then the shattered look when it was "only" Packie Breen, Jim Gallagher, Danny Doyle—the regulars.

By eleven o'clock, the neighbors had disbanded , and Jack had not come home. With mumbled words of comfort, "Sure, he probably just got held up at Dalton's..." each little group wandered off into the inky night.

At about two a.m., the borders started up, waking Myles from a deep sleep. He peeked out the window and could see them in the moonlight, swarming around the road gate. It seemed as if someone was trying to come in the gate, someone they didn't know. Who could be coming at this time of night? This went on for some time, about half an hour; then they fell back, growling and seemingly cowed. Then all fell silent, and Myles fell back to a fitful sleep.

Around three a.m., Myles came suddenly awake with an urgent hand on his shoulder. His mother was shaking him, a strange tension in her voice: "Myles, wake up! Wake up! Will you please come into the other bedroom with me? Your father's been drinking, and I'm afraid." As if he'd been stuck with a hot poker, Myles sprang out of bed. His fearless mother, afraid? He'd never known her to be afraid of anything or anybody in his whole life. What could she be afraid of? What was his da going to do to her?

As he came into the inner bedroom, Myles could hear the borders, back in their high-pitched barking, some joining Ben in his deep-chested growl. Why were they growling at Da? Would they remember that he'd kicked Rover? Were dogs capable of revenge for one of the pack?

That's when all hell broke loose. As Myles shuffled toward the lamp outside the bedroom, he heard his father crashing through the front gate. He could hear the distinctive voice over the din of the borders, shouting in a hoarse, drunken diatribe. Myles fought back his fear, thought he might be having a nightmare, an illusion soon erased by the menacing voice descending on the house. Abruptly, the dogs went silent, a silence that was almost deafening in contrast to the howling chorus of a moment ago.

Then came the hoarse, bullying voice: "Get up, Kitty! Get up and make me my tay! Goddamn you, woman. You bitch...you whore. Why don't you have the door open for me when I come home? I'll teach you to show some respect when I get my hands on you. How dare you humiliate me in front of Fanny Wilcox—a woman who never done you no harm? I'm gonna show the whole cockeyed world who's gaffer around here for once and for all..."

Kitty started to cry, first slowly, in a stifled sobbing; then in an anguished, high-pitched confession, in terror of what was about to unfold. The wailing, desolate sound was unnerving for Myles to hear, all by itself.

"Oh, a Cushla, this is a side of your father I'd prayed to the Blessed Virgin you'd never see. He can be so cruel when he has drink taken. I'm not worried so much for myself, but if he does anything to hurt you, I don't know what I'll do...I just don't trust myself to..."

As the sentence trailed off in a wail, an ear-splitting thud from downstairs told Myles that Jack had just kicked down the sturdy kitchen door, which was never locked. Cowering under the blanket, shivering in fear, Kitty and Myles waited for their fate to unfold. Cursing at Kitty, yelling for her to "Come down, bitch...I'll teach you to..." Myles could hear his father staggering toward the dark stairwell.

Fighting back panic, gasping for breath, Myles's own cowardice struck him, like a sharp kick to the pit of his stomach. What kind of man would be hiding like this? What kind of man would be putting up with this abuse? Had his mammie not just asked him for help? Well, she was going to get it.

A towering rage rose up through Myles's small body at his mother's tormentor. No longer was this beastly intruder his charming, fun-loving da; this was just a nasty, foul-mouthed animal invading their home. All fear and compassion gone, Myles made a decision then and there: This brute was not going to make it up these creaky stairs, even if he, Myles Hogan, had to die stopping him.

In one smooth motion, Myles sprang out of bed, grabbed the old single-gauge shotgun from its rack on the wall, and yelled, "She's not comin' down. If ya want the tay, make it yerself." The words flew from his mouth as though he were channeling a grown man, someone older and braver. He cracked the shotgun, checked the live cartridge—just as he'd seen hunters do before sending out the bird dogs—and stepped toward the stairwell, ready for battle.

Hearing his son's trembling voice for the first time, Jack's whiskey-fueled anger exploded anew. "Ah, the little bastard is going to challenge his da, is he? Well, I'm going to put some manners on you while I'm at it. You've been asking for a good whippin', and now you're goin' to get it." With that, he lunged for the stairs.

Myles pulled the heavy shotgun up to his shoulder, hands shaking as he fumbled for the trigger. He aimed the long barrel at the empty stairwell, yelling at the top of his lungs, "Come on! Ya bastard! I swear ta God, I'll blow yer fecken' head off if ya take one more step."

From behind him, Myles heard his mother's voice, calm and steady now—a complete contrast to the wailing victim of a few moments ago. "Give me the shotgun, Myles, right now, and step back from the stairs." Myles was used to obeying his mother when she adopted that tone; despite his resolve, he reflexively handed over the gun. She motioned him to back up behind her with a quick snap of her head.

A wintry blast shook the rafters, chilling the dimly lit bedroom. Myles recognized that voice, conjuring frightful images: Miss Breen's bloody nose; the cowering Hanningan twins; the dead Tanner. In a flash, Myles's rage turned to fear—fear for his da and the danger he was in. His mind raced. What should he do—beg her to stop? Jump in front of the gun? Start screaming to distract her? In the end, he just stood there, frozen at the terrible spectacle before him as Jack kept stumbling closer to the top step. Too drunk to navigate the narrow staircase, he kept falling down, then dragging himself back up to continue the ascent. He was only one step from the top when he saw Kitty and the shotgun's shadow in the flickering candlelight. Until that moment, he'd kept up the drunken rant. Seeing the gun, he hesitated briefly, then charged ahead with renewed ferocity.

"What a welcome…if it isn't the warrior queen herself? Kitty fucken Commandant Cusack, the pride of Cumann na mBan. The vicious bitch who never quite got what she had coming… I've punched yer silly eyes shut before and will again, just for pointing that fucken gun at me. Who do you think yer dealin' with here? The Tans? Do you take me for one of them eejits you can scare the shite out of with yer fierce fucken stare and general's bearing? Fuck you! I'm gonna teach you who's gaffer around here..."

Kitty's voice cut off the diatribe in that low, calm voice Myles had learned to dread: "No, Jack, that's over. You're never goin' to lay a hand on me again. Not tonight; not tomorrow; not ever! " She said this without emotion, the shotgun steady as a rock, and without taking her eyes off her husband, who stood swaying in the stairwell, still wearing his faded overcoat and rain-soaked felt hat.

For a moment, Jack hesitated, cocking his head to one side— as if considering her words. Then, undaunted, he lurched over the final step, yelling: "Why, you miserable bitch, I'm gonna take that fucken shotgun n' shove it..."

That's when Myles heard the thud of the hammer and saw his father's white shirt explode in crimson across his chest, his body jerking backward into the dark stairwell. Everything went into slow motion. He had lots of time to observe the details of Jack's surprised expression, the wordless calm of his mother's profile, and the seemingly endless racket of the creaky staircase as it absorbed the crash of the tumbling body.

The borders started up again. This time, the sound had gone from the high-pitched bark to keening—all of them in unison, as if on some invisible signal. They were answered across the valley by other borders, keening back, their eerie chorus reverberating around the Sugarloaf Range.

Myles stared in horror as Kitty's right hand slowly and steadily set the shotgun against the bedroom wall. She betrayed not the slightest tremor as she picked up the flickering candle and followed her husband's tumbling corpse down into the kitchen. The turf fire was still smoldering in the grate, and a moaning wind swept down from the Sugarloaf, rattling the ancient doors and window panes. The borders continued to keen as Myles absorbed the horror of the scene on the kitchen floor, the same concrete floor where it all began a thousand years ago on that first magical evening in May.

An hour later, a somber, rain-soaked dawn was breaking over Enniskerry as Myles pedaled his Raleigh across the Dargal bridge, just a mile from the parish priest's house. Still in a daze, head down against the driving mist, he relived the scene in the kitchen: his father's blood-soaked corpse stretched by the fireplace, his mother calmly blowing the bellows as if nothing had changed.

"Mammie, what are we going to do?"

"Go straight to Enniskerry and fetch Father Cavanagh!"

"Right now, in the dark?"

"Right now. It'll be light by the time you get there."

"What should I tell him?"

Kitty slows the bellows, then stops, glancing around the kitchen. The borders have gone silent, creeping into the kitchen, subdued, licking Myles's fingers and lying down in a circle around Kitty, by the bellows. The ticking of the grandfather clock amplifies the heavy silence; hazel eyes meet blue, holding them in a longed-for caress through the miasma of the smoking turf; then comes the calm, dispassionate response:

"The truth. Tell him the hard truth, like the good man you are."

Acknowledgments

THE INSPIRATION FOR MANY OF these stories goes back decades to some of the great Irish storytellers who were guests at our "rambling house" in Ballinvalley, the remote farm where I was raised in Leinster Province. John Brennan deserves special mention for his inimitable rendition of the story behind *Master Carney's Card School*. I'm indebted to Ned Delaney and May Fenlon for their respective roles in *Dreams of Tramore*, and to Ann Morgan, Maureen Keane, Florence Harkin, Kathleen Ward, and Christine Bomba for their unfailing encouragement and sisterly support over the years. And it would be a gross oversight were I not to recognize Captain, my stalwart border collie, the heroic character (and victim) in *All Souls' Day*. I also want to credit *The Boston Globe's* "Spotlight Team" for their courageous journalism in uncovering the abuses of the Catholic hierarchy. Their work, dating back to 2002, provided the initial spark for the lead story, *Rites of Passage*.

More directly, several remarkable individuals deserve credit for giving these stories a chance to be read by a wider audience. Ernest Hekkanen, founding editor of *The New Orphic Review*, accepted *Hard Truths* in full when other editors insisted it be cut back to fit the short story mode. Otto Penzler, series editor of *Best*

American Mystery Stories since 1997, took the story to the next level when he selected it for consideration—and ultimate selection by Robert Crais—as one of the top 20 mystery stories published in North America in 2012 .

For their generous comments and support as colleagues and critics, I want to thank Charles Heckscher, Eleanor Morse, and Padraig O'Malley.

Two of the stories have been published previously. *Hard Truths* first appeared in *The New Orphic Review* (Volume 14, Number 1) in the Spring of 2011; then in *Best American Mystery Stories 2012*, Robert Crais, ed., Houghton Mifflin, and in a very different version, as a chapter in *Far From Land: An Irish Memoir, 2010*, titled—you guessed it: *Hard Truths*. *All Souls' Day* was first published in *The New Orphic Review* (Volume 16, Number 2) Fall, 2013.

As is true of most of my writing these days, I want to credit my mentor, Wayne Johnson, faculty member at *The Iowa Writers' Workshop*, for his incisive guidance in the early going. His editorial insights proved to be invaluable throughout, and there is no doubt he raised the bar on quality. That said, any shortcomings in craftsmanship are solely mine.

Finally, and as ever, I want to thank my wife and lifelong partner, Anne Racer, for her aesthetic insights, editorial support, and steadfast belief in the worthiness of my writing, especially on those days when the blank page looked like the River of Doubt: a daunting, uncharted journey into the Amazonian wilderness.

About the Author

Thomas rice grew up in County Carlow, Ireland, before emigrating first to Sheffield, England, then to New York, while still a teenager. He graduated from Cornell University and went on to a career as a professor and practitioner of sociology. To that end, in 1992 he co-founded the Interaction Institute for Social Change(IISC), focused on social

The author near the Giant's Causeway, Antrim Coast.

justice and sustainability. Since turning to fulltime writing in 2008, he has published several short stories, including "Border Calls," "All Souls' Day," and "The Night of the Arabian." In 2010 he published *Far From The Land,* a well-received memoir about growing up in Post WWII Ireland. In 2012, Robert Crais (as guest editor) selected one of his stories,"Hard Truths," for inclusion in *The Best American Mystery Stories* of 2012. His most recent publication is *Carby's Fate,* a novella based in Kilkenny, Ireland in the late 1990s. He lives in Andover, Massachusetts, and Peaks Island, Maine.

Cover design by Ana Grigoriu

www.ingramcontent.com/pod-product-compliance
Lightning Source LLC
Chambersburg PA
CBHW050843180626
46814CB00007B/2595